The Hidden Face

The Hidden Face

SAMRUDDHI PEDGAONKAR;
NIKHIL SALUNKE

PARTRIDGE
A Penguin Random House Company

ISBN:	Hardcover	978-1-4828-3884-8
	Softcover	978-1-4828-3886-2
	eBook	978-1-4828-3885-5

To order additional copies of this book, contact
Partridge India
000 800 10062 62
orders.india@partridgepublishing.com

www.partridgepublishing.com/india

Dedicated to our loving parents…

Author's Introduction

Samruddhi Pedgaonkar:

I am a simple girl, born in Latur and brought up in Pune city in the state of Maharashtra, India. I am currently pursuing a degree in banking and finance. Writing a novel has always remained my passion and now I'm fulfilling the same. Trekking is my hobby. I also like to read all genres of books. To know more about me, you can connect me through my official author page on Facebook at **https://www.facebook.com/AuthorSamruddhiPedgaonkar** and Feel free to write to me at prsprtpedgaonkar6@gmail.com

Nikhil Salunke:

I am currently based in Pune, pursuing MBA at Sinhgad Technical Education Society. Apart from academics, I am a freelance photographer and a film-maker. I am fascinated by the display of human emotions and love to weave stories around them. However, writing a novel never caught my fancy but here it is; just a sincere try. To catch me up further, you can connect me through my official author page on Facebook, at **https://www.facebook.com/AuthorNikhilSalunke** and you can send mails to me at **nikhilsalunke16@gmail.com**

Author's Note

Based on True Incidence...

           Before you begin reading, we would like to share the story in short. This story is a work of our collective imagination of what might have gone at the back of the incident that shook up the city of Pune. But at the same time, we would like to declare to our readers that none of the characters of this novel share any resemblance with either perpetrators or survivors of the actual event. Our story revolves around the true incident of bomb blast that ripped off **German Bakery in Koregaon Park.**

It's a story which will transport you on a small journey of true love, friendship, expectations, regrets and broken trust. It will demonstrate you that how life crumbles in pieces around you when someone whom you trusted so much turns out to be someone hard to believe in.

First we would like to thank our readers who bought the copy of this book. Your decision to buy our novel means a lot to us. It is a great feeling of honor for any writer when his work is appreciated and respected by readers. We assure you that this book will never give you dull moment.

Sometimes you feel that life is so unfair. But don't have regrets. Life is a one-time offer. Avail this offer to the fullest and till its end. You can't predict what life has in store for you. Even if something goes wrong, don't waste your time in holding regrets.

It's difficult to trust someone who unknowingly becomes yours. Sometimes you are so convinced that you end up trusting a person almost blindly but in the end it is you who gets hurt when your trust is broken, and it happens at a time when you least expect it to happen. This is exactly what happened to this girl, a sudden chain of events unfolding at the speed of lightening left this shell shocked.

Acknowledgements

A special thanks to the whole/ entire team of **Partridge Publishing House – A Penguin Random House Company**, which co-operated and supported us to make our dream come true in a limited time span.

Everyone loves to read. Some of them get inspired by the stories they read and others just continue to read more. But amongst them are some who are inspired enough to start dreaming of penning down something of their own. Writing a book is not an easy task; this is what we have learnt while writing this story. It all starts after having a compelling thought to write a story; you either need some thoughts, an inspiration or exposure to such incidents. And along your journey, as you proceed, it is your imagination facilitates you to shape up the story. The genuine suggestions from your beloved adds up. All of aspects are the pillars of strength detrimental for your story to flourish.

Co-authors often engage themselves in arguments as the writing work progresses. And sometimes it becomes a bit difficult to arrive at a common conclusion all the time. As each of one of you share your viewpoint, convincing your co-author, explaining the grounds for having your viewpoint enriches the overall writing process. We have had our differences as we went on sharing our ideas, paused to discuss advantages and disadvantages of them and incorporated and agreed upon the style of writing.

Samruddhi Pedgaonkar

A very special thanks to my family, especially my grandfather (Devikumar Pathak) who guided me so well, and for his concern support and blessings. My mom & dad were moral support for me always. Then it comes to thank my cousins – Pushkar and Saurabh. After family I was beholden by the special friends who made my dream possibly true. A special thanks to my co-author Nikhil and Varsharani without whom it wouldn't have been possible. Thanks Amit bhaiyya, Smita, Kore, Mone, Swapnil, Anuja, Mandar, Abhishek, Ankita, Pooja, Akshay, Neha, Kalyani and Yashashree.

Nikhil Salunke

First I must say thanks to my parents and Pradip - my cousin, without them it wouldn't have been possible for me to make my dream come true. They were the only one who stood by my side in my good and bad times. My little brother Rishikesh and Uncle Dr. Ambad who never imagined me as a writer but still appreciated my hard work. Rohan, Rucha and Amann who made corrections of each mistake in writing and guided all the time. Sanil, Sayali, Varsharani and Sahar were always there to show me the mistakes that I was doing regularly and they worked towards finding them out to correct them. Asira, Rupa, Shekhar, Heramb, Sadhana, Shweta, Sandeep, Prachi, Jyoti, Tejas, Akshay, Chetan, Aniket, Kaustubh & Shivani were like helping hands for me whenever I shared or asked them about my write-ups, my poems, they were there to provide sincere feedback.

We would like to thank all our friends for their support, those who shared their ideas with us, guided us and boosted our confidence. Some of them even pretended that they were actually listening to our story without showing boredom on their faces. Some were just plain in their reply "Yeah, it's good" without caring to read or listen to it fully. But still their mere presence too was important for us.

Finally, a special and big thanks to our editor Kaumudi for polishing our story. And also the readers, for their love and support.

Contents

Aroma's Café

           When we were walking upstairs, first we heard funky but pleasant and gentle music emanating from speakers fitted in the walls to create an ambiance for a perfect date. The scent of brown polished wall was overpowering. After climbing few more stairs there was a food counter on the left side filled with coffee flavors, you can smell them easily. At the counter, there were innumerable varieties of beans and deserts. Black and coffee brown colored mugs were neatly arranged well on the ledge. The waiter himself was in his crisply ironed uniform, greeted us and asked us to occupy the next couch zone.

There was one intimate couple sitting in the corner. A hot girl had worn a blue one piece barely covering her thighs; her guy was caressing her thighs with his left hand and was simultaneously rubbing her left cheek. The girl was responding by pecking his cheek in return. They were so engrossed in each other's company that if the situation permitted they would have had immediately erupted into a lustful romance. Their bodies were almost clinging to each other, with hardly any distance was left between them. That guy was repeatedly casting a fleeting glance around to make sure that no one was watching them. And whenever he found a chance he kissed her on the cheek and each time she blushed in return. Looking at her response, it was clear that the girl felt enchanted whenever her guy attempted to kiss her.

Pallavi

I am a simple, solemn girl who loves to travel everywhere. My dream is to travel to cover the length and breadth of the country. Somehow I always draws time and embraces each opportunity to explore. I often led the expedition as a trek leader of **MH-Trek Club** of Pune. The club organizes adventurous treks and tours. I am madly in love with the nature as it keeps me fresh and contagious with energy and enthusiasm; all the time. I always waits for the next trek. I had travelled almost 100 forts out of 352 forts in Maharashtra State.

Rohan offered me a seat on the right side of the table and he himself settled at the corner seat. I sat in front of him so I could easily glance outside and catch glimpses of how people enthusiastically shopped on the street and also to check on the couple that was enjoying their endless conversations and engaged in their romance at its best in public. This *Fergusson Street* was one my favorite hangout place. While I was watching outside, suddenly he enquired me, "What are you watching dear?"

I reacted as if someone had scattered my chain of thoughts for a fraction of seconds.

Me: "Nothing, I was just umm…watching at those luxurious cars that are parked at the corner of that lane." I stirred up a bit of restlessness and took a deep breath while answering him.

Rohan: Oh. Is it? You love cars?

Me: Yeah, I love them, especially modified luxurious cars.

But I was thinking something else about how I could tell him. He started sharing his all stuffs about his personal and professional life; but here I am sulking in fear, restlessness and discomfort. When we were trying to get engrossed into our talks, a waiter came to take an order and provided us a menu card. As waiter came between us Rohan was giving weird expressions to him like as if he wanted to ask him; "Why you moron! Couldn't you come after some time?" He told him to wait for another 10 minutes, giving him a smile sarcastically. Waiter left immediately. He asked me if I wanted to eat something or not.

Me: No, I want one regular cappuccino only.

Rohan: Okay. If you want you can; just read menu card once if you like anything you can order. Especially you can order Mojito's if you like. Trust me, it tastes different.

The perfect picture was visible on the menu card itself. Glass has been fallen down; including red wine and one lemon slice hanging on the top of the glass. Those glasses were in the perfect curves, those curves which an ordinary guy tries to find out in girls. That thought put a wicked smile on my face.

Rohan: Pallavi, what will you have?

Me: I want one regular cappuccino with whipped cream and nothing else.

Rohan gave order of two regular cappuccinos.

I was thinking too much. I don't know how this date will go on today. I was waiting for a coffee and simultaneously thinking of telling him everything after having my coffee. I didn't know how I could manage to have an eye contact with him. I was frightened. In between, I was watching outside; just to avoid an eye contact with him. I was least interested in spending time with him; the thought of the same was making me uncomfortable since our first date. I forgot how much I used to laugh. I was so far away from making witty smiles and having fun all time. It was kind of feel like something is missing. I didn't know whether I should tell him or not. If yes; from where should I start? How will he react? I have no answers. Many unanswered questions and negative thoughts were lurking in my mind.

Rohan

It has been 15 minutes we were together but still there was no feeling of intimacy between me and my fiancé Pallavi. I noticed her that she wanted to tell me something as she got engaged in an imaginative fantasy and pretended to be a normal, but she couldn't. Her eyes weren't meeting up with mine from past few minutes. Since our previous meetings, I have noticed that those eyes were broad baskets full of question marks. I wanted to ask her petty many times but I could notice complete denial in her eyes. I didn't have any idea about what she might be thinking. Did she have any intention to tell me? I guess I should broach the topic. It might help me to know what was bothering her.

Me: So how's everyone at your home?

Pallavi: Everyone is fine. And how's yours?

Pallavi

Before I shall answer him; a thought came in my mind that I was asking him unintentionally. There was something else I wanted to tell him but I had no guts to open-up them. I was waiting for the right time. But how should I tell him that was again a big question stroked my mind. The better option was to discuss about our marriage shopping so that it might help me loosen up with him.

Rohan: They are fine. They are eagerly waiting for our marriage. Pallavi, what if both of our families will do shopping together? I think it will be of great help to us to know each other's family very well. I want your opinion.

My reaction shocked him; as if he had asked me for a night out. My face was full of startled expressions and I just wanted to hide it but I couldn't. I haven't reacted for few seconds. I was thinking what my opinion should be? Is he serious? Why he wants my opinion? I agreed afterwards and we started planning our shopping stuffs. I was trying to convert his attention towards me so that I could feel a bit comfortable to share everything with him.

All I wanted was his moral support. I was looking for his trust which would reflect in his eyes. I hoped he would understand me more appropriate. I didn't want things to get affected just because of my past. Waiter came to serve us. The smell of coffee charmed in my nose. While drinking a coffee; we were discussing about the place where we can do our shopping. As Rohan was new in the city he didn't know about the places where girls usually shopped for their wedding.

He was asking me in a very excited tone. He wanted to be a part of my marriage shopping too. He wanted his wife to wear a traditional sari on a wedding day as if he wanted to immerse himself in my beauty for the entire day. He nodded suggesting that he wanted to be with me for his rest of life from right now.

I sensed his love for me even when he was trying to confess it in a roundabout way. He never failed in that. He was a bit formal kind of person; a bit less romantic. He looked too cute when he expressed his feelings. He never failed to seek my opinions. No one can miss sincerity in his words. It's not exactly any different but the way he confessed was very simple and one can find that his words were meaningful. But to be honest; I wasn't in a mood of discussing our marriage shopping. But at the same time, he enlightened my mood so much so that I was ready to share with him.

What can I do but by sitting in front of him with helpless hands and keeping approximately two feet distance between us. What I can do was play but finger crossed game with no opponent to play. I didn't know how to start narrating my entire story to him.

Your mind doesn't work unless you have a coffee; at most of the time when you have so many things eating your head and mind. My fiancée is sitting in front of me, trying his best to give the best companionship to me and all I could do was to watch him helplessly. So many time, I had tried my best to throw away my past from my mind, but it didn't work. Whenever he confessed his true feelings for me or complemented me, I was left speechless.

Sometimes I have a feeling that due to my mistakes in the past, I was imposing myself on him. I don't want to crash our life together just because of my past. I didn't fell in love with him as a person but I have started to admire him. But, I haven't told him yet. I wanted to tell him how he understanding he was. I remembered previous dates with him. It was always so silent, ridiculous and unsupportive. Whenever I met him in the past, I used to behave so miserable. But he never complained. I guess he might have taken it in another way.

"Rohan" I called him. He gave me a surprised look. His eyebrows got perked up as if I have asked him for a fervent kiss. But after some time I realized that after our engagement I have always called him by his name in a very soft tone. I took a sip of coffee and cleared my throat. I wanted him to listen very carefully to understand me very indubitably. I neither wanted to stir up old memories nor did I want to move on without telling my fiancée about my past. If I wouldn't, it would make me feel that I was destroying Rohan.

Rohan

I fixed my eyes on her. When she called me by my name after long time I felt astonished. I sensed that finally she might have come to the point that she wanted to share with me. She did not want to hide it anymore. I don't know what she might have to tell me. Listening to her soft voice had mesmerizing effect on my heart. She looked briefly in my eyes which were catching her lip movement. Her simple and gleaming eyes were the beautiful spot on her body; anybody can stare at them for longer time. She was looking extremely beautiful so that no one could ever get tired looking at her. My phone rang just before she started her narration.

Pallavi

He excused me for some time. Again, my heart plunged for few seconds. How could I muster so much courage again? I was unknowingly sure that Rohan will support me. But still I had this feeling like I was standing at a ticket counter when I had no right to ask them to open the counter to let me buy movie tickets.

I looked outside. Suddenly my eyes went to that place; from where my life has taken me for granted, from where my life had met with a twist. Whatever I was expecting from life that it should inspire me; it should develop a faith in my surroundings. I want to spread the happiness. I want to explore myself. I want to travel through people's minds so that I can help them to put aside their regrets, nervousness and hence it might help me to bring love and happiness in their life.

I wish I could do that. I wish no one could ever face the situation that I had faced. Unwanted thoughts were teeming up in my mind but I restrained my tears. Sometimes life seems so unfair and it fades away with memories leaving behind to keep you twiddled around it.

Rohan

I hung up phone in few minutes to join Pallavi. I noticed her, she was looking outside. She was deeply gripped in her thoughts. I didn't want to disturb her. I took a sit and was only observing her. Her eyes were saying that she needs condolence. Tears started rolling down from the corner of her left eye and it seemed like as if she is going to be burst into tears. As soon as I noticed tears flooded her eyes, I took a tissue paper and held in front of her. But she realized it after few seconds. She noticed me a bit late. She started to wipe her tears hard and fast.

I asked her purposely what the reason behind those tears was. I wanted to know. I can't bear tears in her eyes. She gave a thought for a minute. She was ready to tell me. But before that she asked me to promise her that I will not turn against her. I promised her just the same.

Pallavi

How he noticed tears in my eyes? He scratched his head as if to say that something was wrong with me. He urged me to tell everything and I agreed only after getting a promise from him. I didn't want to let him feel sorry for what I had to pay for in my life. All I wanted was his support.

I took a deep breath. I started narrating him, the story; the past was all about a girl who was heartbroken because of undesired event that had unfolded in her life. She had not have dreamed of having had to face such circumstances in her life. It wasn't something that one will search for solution and besides no one could ever able to afford it.

I don't know how to tell you; it's not an ordinary story. It's something that you'll find detestable. But let's see I'll try my best to share everything with you.

Best Friends Forever...

Memories last forever
never do them die,
a true friend stays together
never says a goodbye...

If someone asks me that how many friends do I have. Then I had an answer; I have only two soul friends.

Yes, it's true. The two brightening stars of my life that were always been with me to brighten my each single dark moment. We all know that every human being in this world has at least one soul friend in his life. The journey to make friends starts from our childhood and it won't finish till the end of life. But in this journey only true friends stay with you from start to finish without expecting anything out of you.

Eesha and Siddharth were the two ever and the best friends I had in my life. Our friendship started from our school days and we would be still together and will always remain. Even destiny would not be able to plan something that will draw us apart.

Eesha

Eesha was a perfect and the most elegant girl. God definitely must have worked little extra to refine her beauty before dispatching her on earth. Eesha is blessed to have pure allured skin, with natural brown eyes and long sleek hair. A little dimple on her right cheek looks perky whenever she smiles. She was a kind of girl with whom anyone could fell in love. She was always the first one to respond if someone needed some help. She was very strong minded girl. She had taught me so many things on how to overcome the challenges in my life. She has always been with me whenever I needed her.

Siddharth (Sid)

What can I say about Sid; he is a true friend who has been always stood by me in my both good and bad days. He was a trusted adviser and helped me to get out from every critical situation in my life. Sid always has a solution for each little problem. He was tagged as naughty boy in our school days but has a very good sense of humor, he could easily read mind. A special quality in him is that before I could even cry out for a help he is already there waiting to help me to find my way through problems.

I, Eesha and Sid are a perfect pyramid of a friendship.

Sid is a very handsome guy with a pale skin and a perfect athlete features and stands tall at 5'9 ft. Flamboyant Sid was known to flirt with the girls in our college days. But he was someone who was always on his toes and would not mind to pick up fights for his friends too.

I still remember, I had been so lazy to attend regular lectures during my college days, things changed only if it had been a trek.

Home Sweet Home

Mom entered in my room; first she switched off the fan. As she saw me lying on bed she started shouting at me; the most irritating episode starts then every morning. Her shrilling voice was extremely loud so much so that our neighbors could easily decipher why she was upset with me.

"Come on Pallavi. Wake up now. You have to reach college at 9am and it's already 8."

Me: Mom just 5 minutes, I am not yet ready to wake up.

Yesterday, I slept late at night. I was chatting with my best buddies. We were making plans for the next day. But, everyone had different opinion and kept on suggesting different places that we should visit. We could not agree on the destination.

Now I don't even remember when I slept while chatting with them.

As I asked my mom to wait for 5 minutes, I took blanket over my head and again slept keeping my eyes half opened. I was extremely heavy eyed. And there I was almost 10 minutes late. I heard my mom screaming at me again; this time it was deadening and I finally had to wake up. She gave me a confronting look. I was smiling at her like a child with an innocent face. I stood up and went to freshen up.

Me: Mom, please make sure that you are making one more dish for Eesha.

While brushing my teeth I looked time and it was already headed towards 8.15am.

"Shiiiittttt…! Eesha is going to kill me now."

Eesha was about to reach around 8.15am and still I wasn't ready. I took my clothes and went straight inside the washroom to take shower. I set a geezer on full hot and 50% cold water. While I was applying body wash, I heard the doorbell rang. Mom opened the door and there she was, Eesha.

Eesha: Hello aunty, Where is Pallavi?

Mom: Hello Eesha; she is still getting ready.

Eesha entered my room and knocked at bathroom door continually for 5 times and warned me to come out in 2 minutes. She went on knocking my door till I did not immerse. As she knew that I won't come early. When I came out and

15

saw her. Her face was red with anger as if her both hands were ready to slap me anytime. I gave her a witty smile and asked her sarcastically when she came. I pretended a question mark on my face as if I didn't know.

She was still standing there; keeping her eyes fixed on me and continued to look at me with annoyed face. I went in front of the mirror and removed towel to dry my hair and simultaneously I was asking Eesha about today's plan. She didn't answer me. I keep my mouth shut. I just turned to look at her.

She was texting someone. It might be Sid, the one she can't live without. She was blushing while texting to him and her blushing face is enough to know with whom she might be talking. She was looking hot, a black beauty. She had worn everything black from head to toe. Her half sleeveless top was not even covering her waist fully. Thank god, my mom didn't notice her dress. She was looking sexy. She had put on red stilettos, which went well with her black attire. She hasn't even forgotten to do nail art. She is someone who naturally possesses artistic sense. She always craved for compliments but never meant to have an attention of people.

Eesha

She is sweet and faithful. Without her, my life is like an empty box. Whenever I needed her, within minutes she'll knock at my door. Whenever I wanted to share something, she would put aside all her work and would listen to me first. I have always behaved like an open book in front of her. There is not a single thing about me which she doesn't know about. Similarly, she too never hides these things from Sid.

Sid

Sid has never failed to confess his love for her. He might be flirt with the hot sluts around him but never ever forgot to tell Eesha how much he loved her deeply. He can't live without partying at least once a week. He likes to meet new people. He likes to make new friends. He is a very cool guy. The unbelievable part was that I haven't seen him in formals yet in our school and college days. He never wants himself to carry formal look. He always teased Eesha by telling her about his new girl friends, just because he wanted Eesha to express her love much more openly. She never felt insecure about him. She always respected him and his feelings for her. Such a harmonious couple I have ever seen. They were genuinely enjoying their relationship. True happiness seeps through every pore; you can't hide it, nor do you really need to make an effort to show it.

Love is what makes you live your life and that's exactly perceptible in their eyes.

Pallavi

I never expected my partner as someone who can't live without parties like Sid. I wanted the special someone to enjoy every lunch and dinner with me. I never desired for those hot girls to die to roam around my partner. I might have felt insecure. I want my partner to make me feel hot in order to get intimate with me. I won't expect expensive gifts, hangouts. I want him to be by my side at the time of my happiness and even in my bad times too. I wanted to imagine only him when my eyes were closed. I would love to be in love with him even in my thoughts.

After I got ready, Eesha and I went to the kitchen. I took one chilled water bottle and helpless Eesha sat on the chair, she was still busy texting Sid. Mom was making dishes ready as fast as possible so that we don't get late for our college. My mom had made *Aloo Parathas* for us. Eesha was having *parathas* with tomato ketchup but she was drawing more attention to chatting with Sid. And finally my mom scolded her to keep her mobile aside as we were getting late and my mom doesn't like to have a food while holding your gazettes in your other hand. She urges us to give attention to people around rather than to your gazettes.

Unfortunately it was already 8.45am. As I see there wasn't any possibility to reach college in 15 minutes. I knew I had missed my first favorite lecture.

We reached our college almost 45minutes late. Sid was waiting near the parking lot. Daily we three used to park our bikes there. When we reached there, Sid was looking at us with annoyed face. I laughed a bit and glanced at Eesha. We went near him and asked about lectures.

Sid teased us and said, "Here are those pretty late comers. I thought you would come without applying a makeup. But you almost took half an hour just to get ready and remaining half hour to reach the college. I am fool who was waiting for you both since one hour."

"I missed my first lecture. You both know how important it was for me to attend. I never missed that slim lady's lecture and I can see her curves only in her lectures. I never get another chance after her lecture gets over. You both even know how much I love Economics. I didn't even find any hot girl here with

18

whom I can flirt at least for one hour till you both came. But I was helpless. I mean I was dying to see you my Persian cat."

Eesha beat Sid, and said, "You bloody cockroach. Stop calling me a Persian cat."

Sid: Okay. Chill. I won't call you Persian cat again.

Eesha: Pallavi, look at him *yaar*. He is calling me a Persian cat again.

Me: Sid, Please stop it.

Sid: Fine. Sorry babes. But I could have almost died here if I had to wait more. But why I moron repeatedly tell you this thing every day from past week?

Eesha hugged him I watched both of them were hugging each other. I came from backside and jumped over them to hug both of them.

We were deciding what to do then. I asked him who's next lecture was. Sid answered with his irritated face. He just told us that he didn't want to attend the next lecture. We both were surprised. We both gave him a defying look. Then he told us that Mrs. Bhagwat Madam's lecture was the next. I and Eesha both laughed in unison.

Mrs. Bhagwat ma'am was a fat lady and was famous for her harsh manners in our college. Sid never dares to attend her lecture. He tries to force us to bunk her lecture each time. His decision not to attend a lecture was unchanging. Of course, Eesha will turn to NO because of Sid and unfortunately I would have to.

I miss my school days...

In school days, both Eesha and Sid were different. Sid was the only one of the best smart looking guy in our school. He was mischievous boy in our school days and Eesha was exactly opposite; a shy girl. She didn't even dare to talk with the boys at that time. Now she has fixed up on only one boy with whom she wanted to have endless talks, and that is her Sid. She doesn't even have so many friends. I used to share the bench with Eesha and there our friendship begun. We used to sit on the last bench from first girl's row. Sid always used to sit on the last bench in the middle row. So that he could quietly glance at all girls in the classroom.

I still remembered my school days. Eesha was so simple, but she was so pretty that anyone could fell in love with her looks. Some girls in our classroom were jealous of her. But she didn't care about it. She used to keep her long hair free. She used to wear a black belt *Maxima* watch. She hated people who stared at her for a longer time. She used to get furious at them so quickly. I was the only one there who can help her to keep calm. She never had a single argument with me even on small things.

One day, when our lunch break finished I found Sid was arguing with her. He fell down on her as his leg got entangled in one of the school bags that were stacked in the alley adjacent to the desks. His apologies did not work as Eesha was so angry that she went on to complain to our class teacher. Somehow I felt it was happening unnecessary.

In the very next lecture, peon came and asked Sid to come in the staff room. He went with disappointed face. He didn't even look at Eesha. When school was over in the evening, Sid came to us and apologized once again. Next 2-3 days, Sid was quite during all the lectures. I found Eesha was noticing him too. She felt bad. She wanted to say him sorry but she couldn't. On very next day, she wrote it on a paper.

> *"Hey Sid,*
>
> *I am extremely sorry. I know mistakes can happen from anyone unknowingly. Please don't feel guilty about whatever had happened. But, don't be quiet like a silly boy. It doesn't suit you. Be crazy always. Please forgive me. I am waiting for your forgiveness and smile."*
>
> *- Eesha*

He smiled after then.

On that day, when our school got over; he asked for a friendship with us. From that day onwards we became friends. We had so much fun in our school but we studied hard. Sid was good at basketball and I was in lawn tennis. We both played in interschool competition. Eesha cheered both of us every time. Eesha wasn't in any sports activity. Many times we had to miss our lectures for sports practice and then often, we used to watch movies and sometimes went for hangout.

We enjoyed our school life to the fullest. We helped each other several times in completing our assignments. Sometimes we used to do it together. Whenever Sid troubled Eesha, she ran to Sid's home to complain to Sid's mom. And aunty used to scold Sid for the sake of Eesha.

I must say thanks to my stars for a good fortune of having friends like Sid and Eesha in my life. We us to cheat our teachers by copying each other's assignments except for the first page on which we had to write our personal details. School days were very precious for us. We never thought of joining each other in college too by choosing the same stream together.

Food Arena

Days were passing like sand slips through hand. We were pursuing degree course. I was observing sudden change in Sid's behavior day by day. He wasn't like before. I thought to meet him personally to ask the reason behind it.

We met at Food Arena. The place wasn't that much crowded. It was pleasant surprise for me to hear Sid's secret. He was in black T with hood and in his comfort blue denims. Sid ordered hot coffee for us.

Me: I don't know Sid. I guess you are in love with Eesha. I felt like your behavior has changed. You're giving so much attention to her now a day. You're engrossed while talking with her or whenever you're with her. Don't you think you're in love Mr. Siddharth?

Sid: Are you kidding me Pallavi?

Me: No Sid. I am damn serious. Please tell me if you are.

Sid: Okay. To be frank, I am confused. I like Eesha. I always loved to be with her whenever I wanted to spend my time with. But I don't know whether I'm in love with her or not.

Sometimes I find myself waiting for her message, her call. Sometimes I crave to hang out with her. Sometimes I get a feeling that I can't ignore. We love to tease each other. It makes both of us forget our sorrow, nervousness. I love her company. Is it infatuation or love? I don't know exactly what's there in between us; but sometimes it makes me do crazy things.

Me: Why didn't you tell me duffer?

Sid: Because I wasn't sure. But when did you notice me?

Me: I knew it. I sensed your change of behavior from past few days. You are so different with her. You can hide it from Eesha but not from me. Eesha couldn't observe it. She is a silly girl.

Sid: Yeah. It's true. But how come will I get to know what it is. Is it love or infatuation?

See you soon...

Eesha and her family were planning to go to USA for three months. When I came to know about this, I immediately informed Sid to notice his reaction. He was so stunned! I did not know he will be surprised like this. He was in love with Eesha for sure; but he couldn't accept it till he himself realized it. I was at her place to help her in packing her bags. Sid wasn't there so I intentionally asked her.

Me: Eesha, will you miss me?

Eesha: Of course. I am going to miss you sweet heart but we will be in touch every day.

Me: And Sid?

Eesha: Sid. I wonder how I will spend three months there without him.

Me: Ohh. I see. Ahem. Ahem.

Eesha: Shut up Pallavi.

I found she was hiding something too. She never expressed what's running in her mind. As usual girls never tell any guy anything straight out anyway; the guy always needs to figure out what's on their mind. But it does never have been difficult to catch Eesha when she tries to tell lies. I was sure that they both developed liking for each other. They both were happy in each other's company. I was waiting for the day when they both will realize that they are in love with each other.

Eesha and I were equally demented. She was having trouble in selecting a dress for her. I acted like as if I was not able to suggest a dress for her. Then I told her to ask Sid. I just wanted to notice her reaction. She agreed so quickly and immediately she sent him a message on Face book and attached two images. Sid selected blue color dress for her. We three idiots were going for a movie and after then for a dinner. I have planned these for Sid, two days prior to Eesha's flight. I thought they both will share their feelings for each other that day but they couldn't. But I found Sid was a little bit nervous.

They both had a chance to express their feelings for each other. I was intentionally trying to tease both of them but they didn't get what I was trying to tell them. The day was so normal, nothing happened as I had imagined.

Sid messaged me in the night to say thanks for the plan. I replied that I had planned more than that but you fools didn't get my intention behind it. After receiving my reply he immediately called me and asked what my plan was. I refused to tell him and hung up the phone.

Sid

We never felt alone in the presence of this guy. He was the only one who was always available to help us, to accompany us whenever we needed him. He never complained about us. If any girl wished for a caring and sweet guy in her life, I would better suggest the one like Sid, a perfect guy. He has everything. He is bold, rich, but it doesn't ever matter him a lot. He always used to stay cool and practical. An emotional quotient in him is absolutely zero. He is a very straight forward guy who wants to be independent in his life.

Eesha told us to come to drop her at the airport. She wanted to meet us again before she goes. That time I saw a strong feeling of hopes in Sid's eyes when she departed as if she is leaving Sid forever. I told Sid now in some days you will get your answer whether its love or infatuation. I hope you will share it with me.

And it was love...

           He was feeling empty without her. He almost spent three months by remembering the journey of our friendship, seeing our pictures of our time together and wishing that she could be with him. His mind had stopped working. He used to be awake till 3a.m. just to stay connected with Eesha. He was waiting when she will come from USA and will confess her.

He wanted to tell her three magical words only when she will be in front of his eyes. He was so much involved in her. When he was sharing this to me I realized he can't live without her. He was madly in love with her and I could see it in his eyes; in his words too. It was love only. He was looking so cute when he was telling how he wanted Eesha to be in his life, how he would treat her, how he would keep her happy through-out in his life. He took promise from me that I won't disclose it to Eesha. I promised him, but I gave a thought that I must help him without letting him know just to get his love for his rest of life.

One night, Eesha came online on face book and I asked her when she was coming. She told me to wait for three more weeks. I was so much happy that days were running faster. But she told me to keep quiet as she wanted to give a surprise to Sid. I felt like someone who has a big donut in her mouth which she was not able to eat it properly.

I was thinking why Eesha wanted to keep it as secret. Is she wanted to surprise Sid? I couldn't read her mind this time.

Coffee Day...

She had a plan to surprise Sid without letting him know about her comeback. Sid was dying to meet her. Sid used to keep telling her every day that do come back as soon as possible. When I asked him to meet in CCD, he refused to come. But, I convinced him a lot. He has another plan but when I told him that I want to share a secret about Eesha he instantly pulled his socks. My plan was almost successful. I was so happy for Sid. I knew he would be surprised after seeing her.

We planned for a very next day after Eesha was about to arrive in Pune. I was excited about what will happen. Will Sid pour out his heart to Eesha? Will he confess his love for her? How Eesha will respond him? Many unanswered questions were running through my mind. I was overwhelmed with so many questions.

As usual Eesha came to my place to pick me. When I opened door I was surprised by looking at her. She had worn a Pink colored off shoulder top and narrow bottom blue jeans. Her hair was little brownish colored and half curly from tip.

I informed Sid to reach at CCD in half an hour. We reached 15mins before him. We took corner side table from which CCD parking can easily visible to us. When I found Sid in the parking and he was parking his moped. I instantly told Eesha to go in the washroom and won't come until I gave her a miss call and she agreed.

Sid called me and I picked a call to tell him to come inside the cafe. He has worn a black-grey shaded Ray Ban glares and white slim fit t-shirt exposing his chest muscles outline. He had worn a *Fastrack* sport watch. His dark blue trouser was very simple and straight bottom. He had worn a pair of brown color woodland shoes. He had kept a slightly visible half shaved look. His body odor so much inhaling that I can guess easily which perfume he might have spread on his body.

When he sat on the chair, Eesha came from behind without making any sound. She slowly come close to him and screamed in Sid's ear. He scared so much that he almost controlled his words. After looking at his reaction we started laughing till our stomach felt pain. He hugged Eesha very tightly; he did not bother about people watching at them. He said Eesha that he missed her so much. There was much more charm added to his words. But Eesha took it casually. She reacted with her gorgeous smile and he stared at her for longer. I chose to keep quiet for some time to observe them. I wanted to look them in each other's arms. I wanted to see them like a snuggling couple. Sid was extremely happy and I too was for him.

Sid cleared to me that he fell in love with Eesha. Sid was thinking to say those three magical words to Eesha but in an innovative way.

The day after tomorrow...

Eesha found a text message from Sid.

> "Hey Eesha, meet me today in the afternoon at CCD where you had given me a surprise. Now it's time to surprise you. See you. Take care."

She didn't ask him any questions. She informed me and I started picturing them with each other and was thinking how their story will start. I knew that Sid was going to confess her. In the evening, Eesha called me to tell me their story.

She was looking so ugly. She was smiling like hell. I haven't seen her yet like this. She was on cloud 9. She was laughing too. Her expressions were like as if she had taken Sid's proposal seriously or not? What would have happened between them? She started elaborating their story.

"Sid was waiting at CCD outside in smoking zone. I went to park my Moped and waved Hi to him. When I waved he stood up and walked towards me. We hugged each other. I found few people were staring at us but I ignored them. I found this hug was special. Sid took me very gently in his arms. I felt the difference in the way he held me today. But I didn't give a thought. He smiled and told me to occupy a sit in the corner. He was calm at that time, there was something striking his mind. He was feeling uneasy.

We almost kept quiet for few minutes when we met. I wanted to ask him why we were so quiet; but he didn't allow me to ask something more. He just asked me what I would like to have, a coffee or something else. First time I felt restless.

I told him to order one cappuccino with whipped cream for me. I preferred to sit quite. He went to place an order and came after 15 minutes. He was communicating something with the waiter. I didn't sense it and neither had I asked him. I found Sid has changed. He was not behaving normally since yesterday, the day I gave him a surprise. I was sure that something is wrong.

Sid stood up and murmured something to the waiter. Waiter smiled and gave him a thumb up indication. Nothing was getting in my head. I preferred to keep quiet. I didn't ask him a single question. All I was waiting for the time he would tell me.

More than coffee...

Sid winked at me. He told waiter to buy some extra white sugar packets. He was laughing while telling me and it was enough to know he was lying to me. But I didn't utter a single word to him. Later he said in a flirty tone that he wanted to add some more sweetness in our coffee. I didn't react. As waiter came he took a trey from the waiter and signaled him to go away. I didn't know why. Sid himself took one cup and put it in front of me and I was totally astonished by his surprise.

I LOVE YOU...

Those three magical words had beautifully written on a coffee using chocolate syrup. It was like I am just imagining in my dreams. I was feeling like as if suddenly my stomach had an enormous vacuum. Sid was looking in my eyes continuously.

I was almost lost my all words. I left speechless and I was still wondering what was going.

He just smiled at me and said, "Yeah its true Eesha. I had fallen in love with you; but never confessed you. Yesterday I was overwhelmed by your surprise. I haven't even felt asleep because of you. Yesterday I was thinking whole night how and when I will confess you. All I wanted to propose you in a simple but different way. So I thought to bring you here. I told waiter to write those three magical words and he did it so well. I don't know what you feel about me or you love someone else or not. But I know I am in love with you and always will till the death does us apart.

You don't know where your love is waiting for you but today I found my true love her; in front of me. I don't know what future can bring for me but I know one thing and I want to live my present and future with you. I knew your decision won't affect our friendship either. But I Love you very very much.

Eesha

His love for me was true. I found honesty in his sparkling eyes and in his words. I didn't know what to say. I even failed to notice that is he waiting for my answer or not. I was just looking at him as if I am dreaming that proposal. My eyes went on those words again.

I moved my eyes to him. He was so quiet as if I had punished him. I knew he was waiting for the answer only. I was thinking how I could tell him "Yes" from my side. Yeah, I used to like him a lot but never tried to pour out as I was scared not to affect this to our friendship.

I took one sip of coffee and said yes to him. I don't know but he is a person on whom I can trust blindly and love infinitely. But I found Sid could be perfect match for me. I am the luckiest one with whom he wanted to stay happy for a rest of life. He agreed his happiness is no more without me. I was extremely happy when he smiled after knowing the answer. It was blissful. We had spent almost 2 hours with each other and when we were about to leave Sid came near to me and softly took my hand in his hand. He left me spellbound in love till eternity. It was real. I felt entering in a new world where only Sid and I exists. No one was there except our love. Our love is the only responsible boundary that lies in us."

After listening to Eesha I was damn happy for both of them. I hugged Eesha very tightly and shouted like kids. I congratulated her and also sent message to Sid.

"Congratulations buddy. Finally you have proved that you have guts. You also make her fell in love with you. That's great. It was unexpected from you. But I am very much happy for both of you. God bless you both. Stay together always. See you soon."

Our Junior college time has been ended and now we were waiting for our college to get start. We had enrolled in Ferguson College. We reached at our college main gate. I took a promise from them to attend all remaining lectures and they both nodded. We were thinking what to do now but no one suggesting a place. Then I told them to go to Vaishali. We headed towards one of the famous restaurant in Pune. It's a famous for South Indian foods.

Vaishali...

We all three musketeers were standing in a serpentine queue at *Vaishali* Restaurant. *Vaishali* is one of the most popular restaurants among the student community in Pune. Being the reputed restaurant there is always rush of hungers. The restaurant is especially famous for *South Indian food*. The taste of the food is so appetizing; *sambar, idli* and *dosa*. When Sid went inside to take token number meanwhile I started gossiping about the girls with Eesha. We were observing their dressing sense.

Eesha: Pallavi look at her belly, the girl who is standing there beside the passageway, in black one.

Me: Yeah..! Woowww that's so sexy.

Look there Eesha, the girl who wore a chopped blue top, look at her earrings.

Eesha: Yukss!! It's looking so horrible. How can anybody wear like this? Doesn't she have a common sense?

We gave hi-five to each other, in that mean while someone came and fallen on my shoulder. Eesha shouted at him, *"Excuse me"*. He looked at me for some seconds. He said sorry and moved away. I ignored him. Eesha was yelling at him. But it wasn't of any use.

Finally when we entered in the restaurant and we were about to occupy our seat but our eyes went as a crow flies on that beautiful paintings hanging on every wall. At some tables waiters were asking orders; some people were discussing very seriously about what food they would like to order. Some were waiting for the order to come as if they can't wait for a minute to have a food. One lady was cleaning a knife and a fork with tissue papers.

We got a seat at the corner side. If you compare, open roof area was so much comfortable than indoor zone. There were so many big and old trees are there, lied in the middle of the place. We gave order of one *Idli Sambar* and two *masala dosas*. Meanwhile Eesha was telling Sid about that incident. While Eesha was telling Sid and for some seconds that unknown guy had come into sight. He was in muddy colored clothes. He was looking tensed and confused. The pain was still bothering me. My mind diverted unintentionally for glimpses of seconds. I didn't know why?

Sid: It's ok Eesha. Calm down. There is always such a rush outside so it happens. That wasn't a big issue either. So chill.

Samruddhi Pedgaonkar; Nikhil Salunke

I agreed to Sid's point and moreover Eesha too. Waiter placed an order on our table. We were eating so fast and while eating we didn't utter a single word.

"Wow. After long time we are having Vaishali's special item." Eesha said.

Sid: Nothing can beat Vaishali's taste.

Eesha: Yeah. It's true. That's why people do wait for longer time.

We finished our snacks and paid our bill. We came outside and went to our college to attend remaining 3 lectures. After that I dropped Eesha at her home.

Eesha called me at evening, to inform me that tomorrow she is going to come with Sid in college.

As usual I was late for college. So I drove little fast and while driving I had put headphones to listen to the music. While passing from FC Road, I found that guy again sitting on a bench near Vaishali restaurant. He was the same guy who had fallen on my shoulder yesterday. He had worn same jacket, black sack on his lap and had put earphones in ear. He was alone. While parking my moped I saw him and I ignored him. Already I was late for college so I headed towards my college.

Eesha greeted me a very good morning and waved hii. She hugged me but my mind was somewhere else. I was thinking about that unknown guy. I found him again at the same place. Eesha sensed that I was lost somewhere else and she asked me immediately.

Me: Nothing much.

Eesha and Sid asked at a time c'mon tell us now.

Me: I saw the same guy who had fallen on my shoulder yesterday outside at Vaishali restaurant.

Sid: So what?

Me: I saw him sitting on bench near that Vaishali. He was alone and listening to music. He had worn the same jacket.

Sid: It's okay Pallavi. Why are you thinking about that guy? Just leave it.

Eesha: Sid is right Pallavi. Leave it. Don't think too much. Come on now let's go. We have to go inside the classroom.

While going to the classroom, I was still thinking about him but after some time when lecture started I forgot about that unknown guy. After finishing all the lectures Eesha and Sid wanted to spend some time together and I went to my home. After some time I got ready. I wanted to go to *Appa Balawant Chowk (ABC)*. It's the place in Pune where you will get all types of books like prescribed course books, books essential for entrance exams, novels, second hand books also and all sorts of stationary stuff is sold here. I wanted to take those second hand books for my first semester. Yesterday madam had told me to bring our own book as she found I was sharing a book with Eesha. She warned me to not to come to lectures until I had bought reference books of my own. I had taken all things that I needed. It was so much traffic that I couldn't resist myself to went home early.

I reached late at home. We all had dinner together. As the time passed, that guy stroked in my mind. I went and lied on bed as I was feeling sleepy. My phone was ringing. I was not in mood to wake up. Eesha was calling me. I received the call even if I was half slept.

Me: Hi. Good morning Eesha.

Eesha: Are you ready Pallavi? I am coming at your home in 20mins.

While talking with her I woke up and tied my hair. I dozed off for two times and for that Eesha yelled at me on the phone.

Eesha: Come on Pallavi; please be ready in 20 minutes. Don't be late. We are going shopping.

Me: Okay. Meri jaan. Chill. I will be ready.

Pallavi

Ohh shit! How I can forgot that today we together had a plan for a shopping. I got ready so quickly but couldn't able to take a shower as Eesha was waiting for me downstairs. I went down and I found Eesha was waiting for me. Then we were deciding where to go first? *M.G. road* or *F.C. Street*.

We decided first to go to *Fergusson Street* as it is heaven for street shopping.. We crossed the *Good Luck Café Chowk* to park our moped in Good Luck lane. The only problem on *Fergusson Street* is that you never get a clear field to park your bike.

The Good Luck Café has always being a landmark on Fergusson Street for decades. It is one of the popular and most ancient Café in Pune. They had maintained their charm. The seating area is vast and spacious. The specialty of Good Luck Café remains their lip smacking *Bun-maska with tea*.

We crossed the signal towards Fergusson Street. It's a one way road and both sides of the road are lined up with number of street shops on pavement selling flashy knick knacks for girls. Each time Eesha goes crazy after she stumbles upon colorful scarf's, foot friendly shoes, anatomically designed clothes, creative hand-bags, many varieties of ear-rings, vivid range of nail polish, wrist-watches, wallets, divergent varieties of tick tackle pins. One often finds paperback books for sell on their footpath itself.

Eesha brought so many things. While continuing with our shopping we ate *masala chopped corns* and drank a special *thick cold coffee*. I didn't buy so many things. Eesha was buying earrings. There was so much rush in the shop so I stood outside on the pavement near a florist's shop. I was admiring distinct varieties of flowers that he had arranged sorting them neatly. Beautiful roses, jasmines, decorative big green leaves, gerbera daisies, bellies per Ennis and blue aster alpines. I wished my life should be like these colorful flowers.

Suddenly Eesha emerged out of shop and sought my advice on which earrings to buy. So finally we came at the place where we had parked my moped and headed for MG road.

Eesha: We will go to SGS mall.

Me: Okay.

We reached there and we were entering into SGS mall. Security was screening our bike and frisked us. Again! I came across the same guy. The same guy had fallen on my shoulder. I saw him sitting on the stairs of SGS mall. Today also he was alone. He had again worn the same jacket; sack kept aside and had plugged earphones in ears listening to the music. Eesha didn't notice him because she was so excited about her shopping. I was standing there and looking at him. Eesha came and held my hand to lead me away, towards *the Westside* brand shop. She didn't know where I was looking.

Eesha: "Ok. Let's go to that shop. I have to buy some shorts and tops."

Eesha was seeking my suggestions about color and if it will suit on her. But I was lost somewhere else. Thoughts were continually running in my head about that guy; who found meditative solace in his own world. Eesha sought my opinion after she tried one top; but without properly looking at her, I complimented her casually.

When she went to try another one she took me along with her in trial room. The top was embellished with brownish colored small flat stones. It had white vest to wear inside to cover the plunging neckline. And it also had knots down below west aligned to the left. She was looking glamorous and was sporting a million dollar smile. Yet she was a simple girl character by carrying this uber cool look. She bought that top, 2 shorts and 2 pair of jeans. She paid the bill and we left for our home.

MH - Trek Club...

Those were the finest days of my life, when we used to arrange treks in our state. Especially to Rajgad, Torana Fort, Harishchandra Forts which stood firm as reminiscent of rich heritage of Maratha kingdom. One day I had invited Eesha & Sid for breakfast at my home. We got bored due to our daily college routine. We all wanted a change and that's why we're discussing what to do.

Suddenly a thought came in my mind, "Trek".

Yes I shouted, Eesha & Sid was looking at me surprisingly. I asked them if we arrange a trek nearby. Both were delighted. They felt that would be a great idea. Suddenly we all started to fix a plan on where to go, and a thought struck my mind if we could go to Rajgad? Eesha & Sid gave a green signal. Couples need such a quiet & calm place to enjoy their enchanting romance where no one could watch them.

I used to go for treks from my school life. And now I am a member of one of the finest trek clubs in Maharashtra. I have created my own website of **"MH- Trek Club".** I took my laptop & opened my website to confirm the members about trek. I have gathered many members within 2-3 years at my trekking tours.

Eesha & Sid were helping me to arrange the Raigad trek on next Sunday. As per that schedule, I sent email to all members. I also created event on Facebook to invite all my friends to join this trek. I was quite happy for next 4-5 days and was busy adding final touches to the preparation ahead of this upcoming camp. Sid & Eesha had gotten busy in distributing the pamphlets in the collage. Till Friday I had confirmed approximately 35 to 40 members. That night, I was busy answering phone calls from the other members, giving them the details about the trek schedule; explaining them how we were going, timing of bus arrival and all other necessary information. Due to tiredness from preparations that stretched throughout the day, I dozed off to sleep around 11-11.30 p.m.

I was checking my cell phone and I noticed one missed call from unknown number. I called back on that number at late night, but no response came from other side. I tried 2-3 times, and finally at 4th attempt I heard a voice.

"Hello"

Me: Ah..! Hello. I got miss call from this number. May I know who this is?

"Umm… Yes, is it Pallavi? Actually I wanted to book a sit for Rajgad trek."

It was unclear voice of a guy. He had difficulty while talking properly. Whenever I used to share information he frequently interrupted me. And he then posed another set of questions mostly the information that he wanted to know. I gave him all the necessary information and booked his sit. A new member got added in my trekkers list -

"Aryan".

Rajgad trek

Finally the day arrived, it was Sunday morning. I woke up at 4.30am. I had asked everyone to assemble at the main gate of our collage sharp at 6am. I got freshened up, and left home at 5.30am. Eesha & Sid were already there. I reached there in next 20 min. as usual I was late.

Everyone was present as decided expect for Aryan. We had to move on time. The bus was also ready, but I decided to wait for few minutes for him. I tried to call him on his mobile it was ringing. But he was not receiving the call.

Everyone occupied their seats. I was waiting outside the bus. Eesha came towards me and asked me to go. But I thought to call him one last time. When I called, I heard someone's mobile was ringing near the gate. I followed in the direction of mobile ring. One guy was sitting at the bench near the gate.

I thought he would be Aryan. He had worn a jacket of brown color and a light blue jeans and one black bag was lying beside him. I asked his name.

He replied "Yeah… I am Aryan." He was the guy who had left.

He said sorry and I signaled him to get in the bus as we were waiting for him and getting late for trek. He sat at the last seat of bus. I felt strange as he didn't show any interest in talking with others. He was just listening to the music throughout the way.

Everyone was interacting with others except Aryan who was aloof looking outside from the window. He not even had a single thought of interacting with others. This journey led us to the most fascinating place. It seemed like an ideal beginning of a vacation as we stepped out of our bus into the natural beauty with bounteous trees, lush greenery that covered the hill slope and the appetizing food had made our day. We were greeted by the sight of early rays of sunlight.

We took a route from *Pal Village*. When we reached and parked our bus at the base of Rajgad. I gave some instructions again to everyone related to trek and about our route. There were new people who came for the first time for a trek. I shared the information about the fort with it's an unknown history. When we crossed the Pal Village I told everyone why we were taking this route.

Paali Darwaja, is the easier route for trekkers. We took almost half an hour to reach at the main door known as **Mahadarwaja**, where I again shared the information about our **Maratha King – Chatrapati Shivaji Maharaj.**

"Rajgad itself means a Royal Fort. It was the capital of Maratha Empire during the rule of Shivaji Maharaj almost for 25 years. This fort is built on the hill called "Mountain of the Goddess **Murumba**". The fort is located to the south west of Pune. There are three traces which served as important sites of activities are known as Sanjivani, Suleva and Padmavati.

You will find ruins of arsenal, temples, granaries, water tanks, residential buildings and state offices inside the fort. Bale-Killa is a must visit place. Shivaji Maharaj, gave this fort the name Rajgad which means King's Fort. This fort remained capital of Shivaji for 25 years prior to his coronation as Sovereign king of Maratha Empire"

This information interested everyone to connect with the fort and its rich heritage.

The first day of trek that began with visiting variety of picturesque sights. Everyone was so much excited and was energetic too. We had covered all the doors of fort.

There were many who had come with their professional cameras. The trekkers turned into photographers got themselves busy in capturing the best possible shots of this enthralling sight. Eesha is so clickoholic that she was continually posing and was getting her snaps clicked in different poses. I was on cloud nine; I was simply overwhelmed with the charged atmosphere around.

Deep silence was undoubtedly the most priceless treasure that nature could have offered; a calmness which could pacify a mental unrest; such peacefulness, which could lead a human mind to achieve the rare state of nothingness. One however feels completely powerless and feeble amidst these mighty creations; bare creatures are exposed to the unusual change of mind and fondness of nature. The entire area was covered with colorful wild flowers combined with clear blue sky and the splendor of the fort was captivating. It was an amazingly beautiful trek, with spectacular views. I wanted to get covered myself in the misty atmosphere.

Aryan was exceptional case. He was the only one who was far away from us. We were still behind. I wasn't expecting that much from him as he wasn't a trekker. He has told me that he hasn't done any trek till yet. He didn't even join all of us for taking snaps. I observed him. He had listened to me carefully only whenever I was giving information about the fort and Shivaji Maharaj. But there wasn't a single smile on his face. I wondered why he had come here. A question stroked my mind. He wasn't even introduced himself to us. I found him unintentionally lost in his own world.

We were enjoying a trek. It was a wonderful morning. We were on the fort which was witness to the battles that fought between Marathas and Mughuals. The battle was held 400 years before against Mughal's. Rajgad was boastfully narrating us the victory of Maratha Kingdom. Even 400 years later, Rajgad was still looking young. In the afternoon time, we decided to have a lunch near the shelter space. Everyone has got their lunchboxes. We sat under one of the solid structure of erstwhile palace. Aryan was not there. He was sitting alone. He bought a Tiffin. I went to offer him to join us for lunch. But he refused. I ignored him and returned to join others.

I don't know why, but I felt so disappointed. Why was he behaving rudely? I was trying to avoid thinking about him, but

I couldn't. Eesha & Sid were enjoying each other's company. They were looking sweet in each other's arms; a lucky snuggling couple.

When we were on our way back home, everyone had a bag full of fun, happiness, mixed emotions. We were still brimmed with the enjoyment while returning to our respective homes. Everyone reminded me to inform them about the next trek. And I appreciated their feedbacks. Our trek ended on a high note because of the nostalgic atmosphere created by songs and conversations with trek-mates. I was happy that at least I could manage to bring smile and satisfaction on everyone's face.

The next day, was a warm welcoming morning after trek. I found a message from Aryan.

> *"Sorry for my behavior. Thanks, it was an awesome trek. Do inform me about the next trek."*

Unknowingly a smile flashed on my face. I don't know why but it made me happy.

Lohgad / Rajmachi

Many weeks passed by; I haven't went anywhere outside Pune with Sid and Eesha after our last trek. Sid and Eesha wanted to spend quality time together. They were asking me the place where they can spend almost one full day or more than that with each other. I wasn't so much aware about the places for couples. I had a big question mark in my mind. I wanted to help them. When I returned back home, I searched places for trekking but that time I was thinking about arranging an over-night trek for Eesha and Sid.

Eesha was equally excited and immediately she asked Sid. They both confirmed their seat. We three decided to arrange an over-night trek. After searching few treks and reading some reviews we finalized the trek; Lohgad and Rajmachi.

I started sending messages and status updates on face book so that trek lovers could get to know about it. That time I was expecting few more members to join us than our previous trek. Also I had also sent mails to the members. I had messaged Aryan twice. I was waiting for his reply.

Trek was the only option where I could meet him. I waited for the next two days for his reply. I was expecting Aryan to come. He replied and gave his confirmation. I was little bit happy. I didn't know why but I guess I wanted to know more about him. I wanted to find the reason behind his loneliness; his rude behaviour.

I found he was still behaving rudely. He was answering to my questions only in a one word. I ignored his replies. First we decided to go to Lohgad. Our plan was to spend a whole day at Lohgad and we were going to stay at Rajmachi. Aryan was still quiet in the bus. He wasn't communicating with the people.

We reached Lohgad. It was located to north-west of Pune. The fort was under the Maratha Empire for the majority of time. Lohgad is the part of Western Ghats. During the monsoon the top point of the fort gets covered with mist and clouds. The roads and trails become very slippery during this time. Bhaja Caves, which was on the way to Lohgad was a pleasant place for trekkers. It was very simple and scenic. There were variety of birds and insects spotted in these hills. Lohgad has a long history with many dynasties like Satavahanas, Chalukyas, Rashtrakutas, Yadavas, Bahamanis, Nizams, Mughals and Marathas. This fort used to keep the private property from Surat and later in Peshwa regime they used this fort for living for some time and built several structures such as big tank and a step-well.

After conducting a trek to Lohgad we were walking amidst breath taking weather combined with bountiful nature trails. Rajmachi is a small village in the rugged mountains of Sahyadri in India. In rainy season, this region looks more beautiful, adorned with silvery waterfalls, streams and lust green forests and meadows. First we need to cross Lohgad to reach Rajmachi. It consists of two forts namely as Shrivardhan Fort and Manaranjan Fort.

There are two forts which were built by Shivaji Maharaj during 17th Century. It is a famous spot for trekking. It is a strategic fort located near two famous hills of Maharashtra, Lonavala and Khandala.

I have a habit of collecting historical information to all the people whenever I used to go for trekking. Its 15km trekking distance from Lonavala and that's about one hour distance only. That's why I decided to visit Lohgad first and then chosen Rajmachi for stay.

At the night time, I found Eesha & Sid were sitting on the rock side of Rajmachi. Suddenly my eyes went to the left. Someone was sitting alone at the edge of the valley. I couldn't recognize so I went close to that person. Aryan was there.

I desperately wanted to ask him. But I had a doubt if he would reply? But I mustered courage to ask him what he was doing there alone.

Aryan: Nothing, just getting the feel of cool breeze that glancing at nature. He replied firmly.

I sat beside him, he was feeling awkward. I asked him to join us; but he denied.

"Pallavi come here", Eesha called me. I had to leave him alone. Eesha & Sid had planned to make campfire at night. I agreed with them and asked everyone to collect some woods and bushes of trees. We managed to collect together plenty of bushes and dry branches of trees. I managed kerosene from *bhutta seller*. After our dinner was over, I selected a place in the center for campfire, neatly piled the dry branches and after generously sprinkling kerosene on it; I flint a fire.

Everybody sat around the fire; we made a big circle. I was still thinking about Aryan. He wasn't there with us. What was he doing alone?

Someone started to sing a song.

"Neele Neele amber par chaand jab aaye….." - a famous Bollywood song sung by Late Kishor Da from movie - Kalaakasar.

Everyone started to clap and joined in to sing the song along with. It lasted for one hour. I heard a soft tune of flute. Someone was playing it so deeply. It was unknown tune but changed the atmosphere with its melodious notes.

We all plunged into silence. I went in the direction of this voice and I was surprised, Aryan was playing the flute. I was astounded for a moment but I kept on listening to his tune. I had never expected him to play flute not even in my darkest dreams.

I heard soft and old instrumental melody was being played at the music player in the café. I was drinking a coffee. Rohan was saying something but I was lost in my past; as I engrossed myself in thinking about Aryan. Physically I was present with Rohan; but my mind was travelling on the tune; in the valley of Rajmachi.

Suddenly the flute sound stopped. Aryan turned back. He saw me and stood up. I clapped and said *"Wow, such a melodious tune, you are nice at it. Where did you learn this? Is it your own tune? Or is it from some song that you already you knew?"*

Aryan: I used to play it from my childhood, my grandpa taught me to play." He replied genuinely.

First time in whole day, he answered me so quickly and with a smile on his face. I was surprised. But the tune had an emotional touch, but no one could guess the tune. It wasn't important that what kind of that tune was; but for me what was more important was that Aryan finally started talking to me and answering me with some interest.

Very next day, when I woke up early by 6.00 am, I saw Aryan already standing over there at the same place and doing some exercise. I went towards him. He was so much absorbed in exercise but was looking very tense.

When I started walking towards Aryan, suddenly Eesha held my hand and took me aside. She wanted to tell me something. She was very excited. I was surprised to see her in this excited mood. I got to know what she was going to tell me but I preferred to listen to her first. She didn't give me a single chance to talk to him.

Eesha started telling about her yesterday's romantic encounter with Sid. They both were in the same tent after dinner.

He put his right hand on her waist and his touch aroused her. When he grabbed her waist; she felt like as if someone's boat is floating in her stomach. Then he held her hand and said those lovely words to her. Those words she always wanted to listen whenever she met him.

Made for each other...

Sid

"You're the first thing I think of each morning when I rise, and the last thing I think of each night when I close my eyes. You're in each thought I have and every breath I take.

Whenever I miss you, I look at the pictures of you to make me feel as I am with you. It makes me want you so much right next to me. My life is perfect with you. Having you in my life makes everything so special and beautiful that all I want to feel.

Hold my hand forever and never let me go till the day I die. I love you very much. I can't live without you. There is only one thing I want in my life and that thing I can describe only in one word, "YOU". My love for you is like the wind, I can't see it; but I can feel it every time. We are together and always will. We are meant to be together. As I had a blind faith on our destiny which will never ever change."

Eesha

When I listened to this, a lovely smile appears on my face. We both were drowned into each other's eyes. There was not the smile on our face. We both were very close that there was hardly any distance between us for the air to pass. Our lips met. We had a passionate kiss. He licked my tongue very softly. Our love has reached to colds of the mountains, the vastness of the sky and our energy radiated everywhere. I can surely say that our love is for eternity.

When I was listening to Eesha I couldn't pay attention anywhere else. All I was observing her happiness. I noticed her madness; her love for Sid. I can surely say their love will last forever. His love made her scars vanish for lifetime.

But, where was Aryan?

In the evening, we headed towards our home. It was difficult to ask him in the bus. I thought to ask him when we will return back. I wish I could have made an excuse. But everyone was telling me how they enjoyed the trek.

Pune...

If you want to know the history of India, I must suggest you to begin with **Pune – A Cultural Capital of Maharashtra**. It was known as a capital before 300 years, when Peshwas were the prime minister of whole Maratha Empire.

Peshwas were one of the finest warriors for Maratha Empire, elected as a prime minister. Balaji Vishwanath, so called the first ever chief administrator of Pune city, who especially had a big hand in the development of Pune city. A Peshwa is the ceremonial name for modern Prime Minister who built the famous historical monument called Shaniwarwada, which served as the administrative headquarters during Peshwa regime.

Maratha Ruler - Shivaji Maharaj created the Peshwa designation during the expansion of the Maratha Empire.

The Peshwas were ministers or chief executives to the king. The word Peshwa is from Persian. They were also known as kings. Peshwa is found both among Chitpavans, Deshashtas and Maratha Brahmin communities. Peshwa's were awarded royal status in 17th Century." Kasba Ganpati temple of lord Ganesha, which is based in the Pune city, was built in 16th century in the time of creation of Pune, by Rajmata Jeejabai; mother of Chatrapati Shivaji Maharaj.

Pallavi

I was reading a book. But I was struggling to know something about Aryan. I wanted to call him but I disconnected call for 5 times. Should I call him? If he had asked me the reason why I had called him then what would I say?

His phone rang; but he did not receive the call. Again I called him for the second time. He rejected my call. I didn't know why but I thought he might be busy in his work. So I didn't call him again at that time. I thought he would call me back. I waited for 2 hours; but he couldn't, so I messaged him.

Me: You there? Why you didn't receive my call? Please reply.

Message sent.

I was waiting for his reply. 25-30minutes passed but didn't get a lone reply from him. I went in the kitchen to have a dinner with my family. I was having dinner. Dad was beside me. They were inquiring me about my college lectures and studies. I was answering them casually; but in my mind thoughts were running about Aryan. My mind was pulling me again and again to get engaged in having attention to these thoughts.

After having my dinner I went inside my room and instantly checked my mobile. I had received one message. It was Aryan's reply.

Aryan: Yes. I was busy.

Me: Ohh. Sorry. Did I disturb you?

Aryan: Not at all. Say.

Me: Okay. Nothing much. You didn't tell me; how was your experience so I thought of asking you.

Aryan: It was nice.

Nice? That's it? I was expecting much more from him. But he denied sharing something more.

Me: Okay. Cool. So, what's going on? What's your plan today?

I was pretending myself okay with his response.

Aryan: Not decided yet. I didn't know so much about this city. So it's getting difficult for me to decide where to go.

Me: If you don't mind I can help you. Shall we meet?

Aryan: Why?

Me: Actually, I wanted to meet you. I wanted to know how you felt while on the trek. It's important for me. Everyone shared their feedback except you.

Aryan: I told you. It was nice.

Me: That wasn't enough for me. Please meet me at 4pm at C.C.D. on Fergusson Road; which is near to the same place where we all met for a trek. I will be waiting. Bye. See you.

I took a pause for a minute. I took a sip of coffee. Rohan ordered one more coffee for me. Rohan asked me what happened then. Did he meet you or not?

I don't know why; but I wanted to meet him. I was waiting for him in the café. But he didn't come that day. That was the first time I could have waited for someone for longer time. I was at the café only; was hoping to meet him.

We met next day. He asked me to meet a very next day. He even apologized for keeping me waiting in the café as he had taken it so casually. That night when I informed him that I was waiting for him till 9pm. Then he was so embarrassed. And he asked me to meet a very next day at the same place.

Meeting him was...

Yes we met. I was waiting at CCD. I messaged him that I have reached there. Please do come. Instantly, I got his reply. He was on the way. I have waited for him since half an hour.

We exchanged smiles. Before I could initiate conversation, he apologized me again in a low tone and asked me why I wanted to meet him.

Me: Hmm. Actually I want your help.

Aryan: My help? You need my help? Why?

Me: Yes, your help. Be relaxed. Actually I am confused where I should arrange the next trek. Suggest me some places.

Aryan: But you know very well that I hadn't done any treks before. I came here in Pune for some work. How could I know the places for trek?

Me: Yeah. You're right. Actually I want to help Eesha and Sid also so that they could spend some quality time with each other.

Aryan: Then, why you don't try to arrange an overnight trek?

Pallavi

While talking with Aryan, I was not confident because I lied to him. I was feeling myself awkward. I didn't want any suggestion from him. I just wanted to meet him that's it. But his idea wasn't that much bad. I decided to give a thought about it.

Me: Anyways. I will tell you once I'll had talk with them. But first tell me what would you like to have?

I interrupted our conversations. I went to give an order. I ordered one regular cappuccino and Irish coffee for him.

A waiter served a coffee on our table. I am talking with him but he was still quiet and only responding to whatever I was asking him. I was continuously chattering. But he shared his experience to me. That was a divine feeling he ever had after so long. We almost spend one hour there. He asked me in scornful voice; *"Shall we leave?"*

I wanted to refuse but I couldn't. Unfortunately I had to say yes and he directly went away without saying anything. It just started with a coffee date.

After I met him; there were so many questions raised in my mind. Why he was so rude? He wasn't habitual. What can be the reason behind it? Is there something that took him on wrong track? I don't know but unknowingly I was getting filled with intense desire to know about him. As he was new in the city I made a plan in my mind that I shall explore Pune to him.

Two weeks had gone. My exams were there. I wasn't in contact with him. After my exam got over, we had a party in the night. I missed Aryan. I wanted to invite him but I didn't. Two days later, I had called him. His phone rang. But he didn't respond. I called him twice again but no response came from his side. I dropped him a message. I got his reply in the evening.

Aryan: Why were you calling me in the morning?

Me: Yeah. Tomorrow I am going somewhere and I want you to come with me.

Aryan: But where?

Me: You just come with me. Don't ask me any questions.

Aryan: But why me?

Me: I don't know. You just come. I will pick you at CCD where we met last time.

I don't know he would come or not; but very next day in the morning I got ready; I had decided to take him to visit *Shrimant Dagadusheth Halwai Ganpati Temple*.

Shrimant Dagadusheth Halwai...

I was confused what to wear; I opened my cupboard and checked out every outfit. I selected sky blue Punjabi dress. I took the key of my moped and left from home.

Before leaving I had dropped him a message. I reached at CCD. He was waiting for me. He reached there before me. We waved Hi to each other. He came; and sat on my moped without uttering a single word. He was comfortable. There was least distance in between us.

I glanced at him in the mirror; he was surveying the places, the people. We entered in most crowded place in the city. I parked my moped in the adjacent lane and told him to come with me. We were going to Shrimant Dagadusheth Ganpati Temple. I wanted him to show how people have faith in Ganpati; from whom they want to shower blessings on themselves.

Faith stimulates the responsive grasp of humanity to realize its spirituality that we are all the children of God. This temple is popular all over Maharashtra State. The temple is visited by thousands of devotees every day. The Halwai Ganpati Trust provides housing and education loans and ambulance services to poor and health clinics from donations they receive.

I was waiting in the queue and was about to go inside the temple. But I found myself alone. He was standing like a statue and seemed so surprised. I walked out away; broke the queue just to bring him along with me. But he refused to come and neither could I force him. He stood their only; 25 feet away from the queue. I told him to wait near my moped.

I went to take a dish of offerings which is known as *puja thali*. Turmeric and vermillion were placed to the right of the worshipper and lowers, one small garland, durva, patri that were placed to the left. The unbroken rice is to be placed in the center of the *puja* platter. Wherever you stand in the queue, you'll find the collection box to collect the generous offerings made by devotees, the box especially named as "*dakshinapeti*".

I entered the temple. When I stood in front of lord Ganesha I was feeling so calm and quiet. I bowed down after offering the flowers to Ganesha. In doing so, these puja thali is supposed to acquire the blessings of the god. All these components are an effective medium for transmitting the spiritual frequencies towards the worshipper. The priest collects flowers, garland from those plates and coconut from the earnest well-wishers and then offers this to deity and they cup their down-turned hands over the flame and then touch their palms to their forehead. And then several kinds of *prasada* like *coconut, kesari pedha, tilgul* is distributed to the devotees.

I love to visit the temple in the morning especially on every Tuesday, at Dagdusheth Ganpati temple. Devotees from all corners of the state come to see legendary, wonderful, miraculous and auspicious Shrimant Dagdusheth Ganpati. They congregate here. They worship with full faith in the lord Ganesha and purify their soul. Some devotees pay visit to just observe the idol of lord Ganesha with all the faith and affection.

Aryan was standing near my moped, looking here and there only. With beard he looks so stud. But I never saw him out of his messy mud color jacket; his brown sketchers and a silver locket which has two tubular shaped eyes with short, curved and downward facing beak.

Me: Why you didn't come with me inside the temple?

Aryan: I don't have faith on any deity neither do I believe in any religion. Humanity is the only religion, I always wanted to believe to get and give respect to someone.

Me: But why?

Aryan: It's none of your business. If you have told me first that we were going to temple, then I wouldn't have come with you.

Me: Why? Why are you so reserve minded?

Aryan: Leave it. You won't understand. Let's go.

He shouted at me. How he can say it was none of my business. I walked straight away towards my moped without talking him. I started my moped and we left.

I was dropping him at the same place. He apologized to me for his rude talk.

Me: It's Ok. Don't say sorry. But don't ever do that again. You know Aryan I love historical places. That's why I love to do trekking. Behind every mountain there is some history. You know Pune is considered as the Cultural Capital of the State Maharashtra. It was the first capital of the Maratha Empire under *Chhatrapati Shivaji Raje Bhosale*. In the 18th century, Pune became the political center of India and sub-continent as the seat of "*Peshwa*" who were the prime minister of the Maratha Empire.

Me: Do you love such historical places?

Aryan: No.

We reached at the place where he told me to drop. He got down from moped and said bye to me. He didn't even talk with me more at that time. It was disagreeing.

I was busy in completing my submissions. Eesha and Sid were with me. After completing our submission I told Eesha about my meetings with Aryan. She was astonished for a moment. It was the first time I hid something from her and shared to her a bit late; but, she didn't mind it.

We were completing our assignments for 18 hours continuously. Everybody was at my home for completing submissions. When we took a break to have a coffee at 3a.m. Eesha, a drama queen; who told me to write her remaining write-ups, but I refused her. But she succeeded in blackmailing Sid. Poor Sid, instantly got ready to write her last three pages. Finally we completed it at the early morning. We were so tired; we went to sleep but were unable to sleep because we had to submit our assignments. After submitting our assignments, we didn't attend other lectures. Instead we went back to our home and slept.

I called Aryan but he rejected my call. I messaged him but he didn't reply. Then after some time in the evening I called him again and at that time also he rejected my call. I don't know why.

Japanese Garden...

When I woke up in the midnight; I found Aryan's one missed call to me. But I didn't give him a response because it was too late. He might have slept. I thought to call him in the morning.

Aryan: Hello.

Me: Hello. Sorry, you called me yesterday; but I was slept so couldn't receive your call.

Aryan: It's ok. But you called and messaged me that am why I called you back. I was busy. Why were you calling me?

Me: I want to ask you that are you free in the evening? I want to take you at *Japanese Garden*, if you don't mind. There is no lord whom you will refuse to visit.

Aryan: Where is it?

Me: Not more than 10kms away from FC Road.

Aryan: Okay. Please send me the detail address. I will come there directly.

I wonder why he wanted to come directly. I didn't ask him. I sent him the address and told to come at 4pm. I reached at Japanese Garden a bit late and I saw Aryan was waiting for me near the entrance at main road. I paid for two tickets and gave smile to Aryan.

When we entered in the garden Aryan was looking everywhere. I observed Aryan; he was feeling calm, quiet and nice. He loves quiet places; anyone can notice by looking at his expression.

Japanese Garden is also known by *Pu. La. Despande Garden*. It was full of well manicured lawns, little streams of water flowing by in such a shallow pools filled with round pebbles, little bamboo bridges, benches that were made with the use of bamboos, a tiny and elegant but small waterfall, a small lake with two ducks and many colored fish were swimming in the small pond, a high point which gives a view of the park all around. It has tall trees all along the periphery and bushes and trees that were pruned into fine shapes. There were joggers and sight seers like us who were getting in everyone's way. After spending some time there; we decided to come outside Garden to have some food; and while I was walking towards my moped he called me. He was thanking with smiling face and I gave smile in return. I saw him smiling first time and was looking so delightful.

Meanwhile I had almost forgotten to hang out with Eesha and Sid. I made many excuses to spend time with Aryan.

Intentionally with Aryan...

Koregaon Park known as eminent area famed hangout for rich with such huge varieties of lounges, pubs and eateries; such as Bashos, Carnival Pubs and one of the most prominent place was also located where people flock in was - *German Bakery*.

Koregaon Park was one of the well-established areas in Pune and the fast turning into a commercial marketplace of the Pune city. Many cosmopolitans used to live there. I and Aryan had spent much time over there. I remember that evening I was with Aryan. We were walking from North Main road of Koregaon Park. Aryan was craving for food and he asked me, *"Shall we go to German bakery?"*

I agreed. We went to a place which was laden with romantic and sumptuously rich atmosphere. I still remember; there was a big crowd hanging out outside the bakery in the queue waiting for their turn. But we were lucky; we grabbed a seat within 15 minutes.

Lots of people from different communities and countries used to come there; to have Cole-slaw burgers, chicken rolls and its special item hot chocolate etc. We settled on two low seating chairs and a table at the corner of the left side.

Aryan was gazing at the people from the Osho Ashram; who sat beside our table. They wore their ashram robes which were red colored long Kurtis. They were disciples or volunteers at Osho ashram, which is well known meditation center of Spiritual master Osho. Osho Ashram is named as Meditation Resort which reflects the unique combination of mediation qualities. It is a place where the mind, body and soul can settle down harmoniously together rather than pulling themselves in different directions.

I had ordered chicken roll for Aryan and a hot chocolate for me. I hate non-veg food. But I knew that Aryan definitely would like chicken roll. He was observing to all his surroundings as he was new to the place.

It was a sound of different waves. I didn't know what that was. But the distance between us wasn't so much like before. There was a sarcastic change. I was feeling the different breeze when I was beside Aryan. He was never been expressive to me. But what I thought was staring at his gloomy eyes for longer period.

Me: What are your future plans Aryan?

I asked him unquestionably

77

Aryan: I have not decided yet. I had just completed my B.E. in Mechanical. I didn't get any opportunity neither I was looking for a job. Besides I was thinking to complete my martial art course first and after that I don't know what will happen. Destiny already had planned for me I am just following wherever my path desired to go.

It tastes nice, he replied while eating. I paid the bill and we were coming outside from the bakery and suddenly his cell rang. He excused me for few minutes. I saw he got panic. I went towards my moped which was parked in adjacent lane and I told him to come whenever he was done with his call.

When he hung up the phone he asked me to leave as he wanted to go for an important work. I asked him if I can drop him wherever he had to go; but he denied. He waved me a bye; didn't utter any word and went towards the auto rickshaw stand and vanished within few minutes.

I was confused as every time whenever I met him, I found Aryan in some different mood. I was unable to find what exactly was going in his mind. I thought of spending time with him to help him explore the city as he was new but he didn't care. I tried to call him but his cell was getting switched off.

I came home directly from there. It was almost 9 p.m. It was a Sunday and I used to spend a dinner time with my mom and dad every Sunday. I was nervous for the way Aryan behaved with me but I didn't want to spoil my time with mom and dad.

When I entered in the home, I put aside the thought of Aryan. Dad was watching news on television and mom was busy in preparing special dish for us. I went to freshen up.

A thought kept coming in my mind about a guy who was known to me for last 3 weeks. Why I am so much bothering myself in exploring the city to him even if he didn't care. Am I attracted towards Aryan? Why I am thinking about him all the time? Why I always try my best to help him?

How someone can be so special so accidentally? I asked myself for 100 times. But I had no answer. Instead of thinking too much, I went to the kitchen to help mom. The hunger filled my stomach when I smelled *daal-khichadi*.

I was chit-chatting with dad while having dinner. My dad was like my best friend. I used to share everything to him. But that day I was physically present in front of my parents but my mind was hooked with thoughts about him.

After dinner I was thinking to go for a sleep, thoughts were running in my mind. I lied on bed and had a thought of calling him.

I wanted to know why his behavior was so strange. When we went to Dagdusheth Ganpati temple, he didn't come to me inside. He looked like he has had suffered lot of consequences in his life and that's why he might have done it purposely. I slept while thinking about him.

Have I lost my mind?

My mobile rang and I thought it would be Aryan. But I was wrong. It was Eesha who was calling me. I sensed that I didn't meet them from past few days. I made many excuses to spend time with Aryan and for that I bunked many lectures even without letting them know. How this could happen? How can I ignore my best buddies just for a person who entered in my life few weeks before? I imagined how Eesha will react to me if she gets to know the truth. But, I have to tell them what I have done.

I received her call and we decided to meet in the college.

When I was entering inside the parking of our collage, I found Eesha and Sid were sitting together on the bench beside the gate. Both were staring at me surprisingly and were laughing.

I waved them hi but none of them waved me back. I realized that they must be angry with me and they had to be.

Me: I am sorry guys; I couldn't meet you for few days.

Eesha murmured something in Sid's ears. Sid gave surprised expressions and instantly stood up in front of me.

Sid: Ohh. Congratulations Pallavi.

I was surprised for a while and asked him why so?

Sid: Don't act like a kid. I heard that you have finally found your love.

I was astounded for a moment. I wasn't expecting this from them. It was unpredictable.

Me: What the hell are you talking, Sid? I don't love Aryan. He is just friend.

Sid: But I didn't utter a single name.

He laughed while looking at me. Eesha was staring at me as if they had caught me. They were just cross checking me. How foolish I was. I realized that how they would know about my meetings with Aryan, but I uttered his name unknowingly which made them put a doubtful finger on me.

Eesha: Where have you been from last ten days Pallavi? You didn't even pick up our call.

Me: I shall tell you later, Eesha. Don't think like Sid.

I pushed him away. They saw how I embarrassed was I! They thought that there must be something that I was hiding from them; but they made me comfortable and encouraged me to share with them. I have told them about how I was deliberately spending time with Aryan. Whatever it is I was trying to figure out the reason behind his rude behavior. And meanwhile I started liking him.

The truth is…

Aryan was new to the city. So I was just with him for few days to help him to explore the city. We became good friends. But you both are my best buddies and I promise, henceforth I will never ignore you both.

I was thinking to share my thoughts with Eesha. But wasn't sure from where to begin. I told her everything from the day when I saw him at SGS Mall.

Eesha was like what the hell that I have got messed up with his thoughts. She asked me several times that have I lost my mind? But I was feeling limitless with the one with whom I was spending my time with. I wasn't sure what that feeling to be called; but I wanted to hold myself spellbind with it. I wasn't saying I could have lost myself; but I wanted to lose myself with the time whenever I'll be with him.

I didn't know what he thinks about me but all I wanted to do to let him think about me. It was an intense but short-lived admiration for him. Sometimes I feel like I wanted to wrap up myself in his arms. I wanted to stay like a shadow who would always follow him. All I wanted to bring change in my life.

Eesha: Pallavi you are madly in love with him. I wasn't expecting this from you. You never hid a single thing from me and how could you dare to hide this? And Pallavi what about him? Have you ever thought what he wants? Have you asked him; if he had any feelings for you?

Me: I don't know what he thinks about me. I was getting involved in him unknowingly; but I didn't even know what his feelings would be. May be he considers me as his girlfriend or may not be. I didn't ask him. I didn't even pour out my heart to him. He always seemed new and kind of stranger to me. But he isn't an itinerant person either. And I always find myself thinking about him. He never behaved with me in the way I expected. Neither had I found feelings for me. He always treated me like a friend.

German Bakery...

Sid was asking us to plan something to spend a time somewhere so that he could feel relax. Even I wanted some mental peace. I was in bit confusion about having Aryan in my life or not. I was trying to find out the answer but sometimes things don't allow you to decide inherently. We had no idea where we were going to plan to go. I was lost in picturing my date with Aryan in German bakery. Eesha was astounded and was wondering where my mind was blowing in intimate scenes. She scattered my mind by pinching my arm sharply and asked me to suggest any place. Without listening to her fully two words dropped down from my lips.

"German Bakery"

They agreed to go to German Bakery. At the time of sundown we were going to German Bakery. All I was completely lost in the memories aback of the day I was with Aryan at German

Bakery. It was the delightful noon I must have spent with him. We ordered three hot chocolates.

I was trying to find the conclusions from his words. But he was so smart. He never showed what was running in his mind. He used to hide the things and was pretending like as if there was nothing. I wanted to know what he feels for me. But his rude behavior stopped me from asking him.

Lake City...

        I forced Aryan to go for a long drive. We had planned to go to Lake City - Lavasa. Lavasa is a private city being built near Pune. Lavasa leaves you spellbind with the pleasant weather which makes it a perfect holiday destination in the Mulshi valley of the Western Ghats. I didn't know he will agree to come. I was discussing my future plans with him. But he wasn't listening to me. He was looking down to the endless point of the river; again lost in his own world

Me: Aryan, are you listening to me?

Aryan: Why are you discussing all this with me?

I was confused. I took a pause and decided to tell him the story that I was hiding from past few days. But I found it difficult to pour out all.

Me: Look Aryan. I don't know what destiny had planned for me. I always ask a wish for me that destiny would always be with me so that I could find a single drop of happiness and would share it with the people I love.

I don't know what I was doing was right or wrong but I always had a thought of being with you. I always waited for the time I could spend time with you only. It's true that I have started falling for you. I am sorry I hid this thing from you. I have decided not to confess.

I brought you here just because I wanted to find a peace with you, a place by your side. I had a thought of wrap up myself in your arms. I have imagined all this whenever I was with you but never able to pour out my heart to you.

I Love You."

I found myself dreaming of confessing my love to Aryan. I wish it could have been possible in reality. When I went to the college I was discussing with Eesha about the studies and exam dates. But my mind was pulling me to jump in those dreams again and again. I refused to share them with Eesha.

But I couldn't hide from her. I shared my yesterday's dream and everything from starting about Aryan. She listened to my every word carefully and helped me to let me know whether I was doing right or wrong. She advised me to concentrate on the studies. She has always guided me, how to treat people in this type of situation. She was so balanced. She told me all the positives as well as negatives.

Somehow I was feeling low. I was thinking how to attempt to derail the negative thoughts. Eesha sensed that and as usual she started finding a way to put my negative thoughts aside so that to cherish the moment as we used to do.

M. G. Road...

To change my mood Eesha texted Sid to join us at Marz-O-Rine in the evening at around 6p.m. Marz-O-Rin is a rustic cafe, ideal for hanging out with your friends or having a chit-chat over coffee on M.G. Road. Marz-O-Rin stands as a timeless landmark which offers yummy and affordable snacks. This place is a great one to hang out with a group of friends when you have entire month left and too little money to spend. An indeed legendary place that gives me a feeling of going back and admire the architectural creations of the British time.

We entered in the Mar-Zo-Rine; there was a big rush at the counter. They have varieties of menu right from burgers to sandwiches and from coffee to cool drinks, thick shakes. Sid asked me and Eesha to occupy the table. He went to the counter to place an order. I asked him to get one *Cheese Spaghetti* and *lemon chiller*. We have got a sit in the outside seating, like balcony type area. The outside seating is on the first floor in a balcony area is quiet peaceful where you can see the busy road while quietly enjoying your food. After 15 minutes Sid joined us with the food; as it is a self-service eatery. We were so hungry that we instantly started eating foods.

Later we were discussing about the preparation that we need to do for our exams. But Sid changed the topic and he started recollecting our memories. I remembered the place where Aryan had met me on this precious day.

We all went to M.G. road to celebrate a Christmas Day. Many people from different communities had joined together for this festival. People used to visit St. Xavier's or St. Mary's church first and then went to hang out at camp side area.

Christmas is celebrated to remember the birth of Jesus Christ, Christians believe Jesus was the Son of God. Those days have gone when once upon a time Christmas was celebrated by only Christians. Because of the liberal views that urban people in the cities hold, this festival has slowly found a place in each heart and home of many non-Christians too. It has become a joyful festival for all, as an occasion for rollicking. This festival serves an opportunity to bring people together.

Christmas is something which I feel like to grow up with. In fact, even I don't follow all traditions, but I always look forward to go to cathedral at least once in a quarter. I force my mom to decorate a Christmas tree this time in my room and also asked to bake a cake in the evening. I wanted to feel like having and celebrated. Once I saw a girl who hanged her red socks in the room and had put her wish list in the socks to get those gifts accordingly. We had planned to attend the midnight mass at a church and then to hang out in the camp side area.

When we entered in St. Xavier's cathedral; most of the people were lighting a candle and was murmuring something. First I went to light a candle and kept there at the place where everyone was making the space. After me, Sid and Eesha were gone together to light a candle and I was standing at the corner.

I was watching at the gate where the statue of Jesus in a small hut; who bent on knees and was sharing a food with a kid. There was a person who stood at the gate and constantly watching at that statue. I recognized by his dressings; he was a man. But his face wasn't clearly visible. But he resembled with one of my friend.

When I had went to him and put my hand on his shoulder. I froze for a while. He was Aryan. I was surprised by seeing him at there and equally he was. Few hours before, he had denied me to come with us for celebrating Christmas day but at that time he was in front of me. How?

Me: Hey, what's up? What are you doing here? Why you denied coming with us then?

Aryan: Nothing much. Just I was getting bored at home so thought to go somewhere.

Me: Okay. Come on, let's join us.

I held Aryan's hand and took him along with me. Eesha and Sid were surprised.

Aryan: Who are they?

Me: Eesha and Sid.

They all exchanged smiles. Aryan was waiting outside at the entrance. And we all three musketeers were inside the church. Eesha understood when I signalled her that he won't come inside. We headed towards M.G. Road.

A Christmas event has been planned in the camp every year. Many Santa clauses were about to come over there to add extra sugar in the sweets. Of course, they wore a long white beard, red colour dress and cap with the bag filled with gifts. They arrived in a horse carts and throws away some gifts towards the public beside in the lanes. Those lucky ones receives gifts from him; like we see those people sat in the stadium, feels lucky who succeeded to catch a ball shot by any batsman in cricket matches. Most of the teenagers used to wait eagerly for the Santa. The shops and malls in the city are also flooded with attractive gifts which give you many offers on an occasion to please your friends with goodies. The basic idea is to have fun with the bunch of customers. They sells attractive props also like *horns* – a pair of curved and pointed tool that has to wear on head; *cornets* - a musical instrument with a funny and harsh tone; has a narrow tube and a flared bell and is played by means of valves; and *Santa masks* etc.

We went to Marz-O-Rine and had chocolate rum balls, macaroons, burgers and butterscotch thick shake. Aryan too enjoying was with us. He sounded different. It was easily noticeable that he was delighted to celebrate amongst us.

Night-walk...

We had our first night walk in Koregaon Park. Sid & Eesha wanted to go for a party but I refused to go with them. I was discussing my future with Aryan. He was listening to me carefully.

When I had first heard him playing flute, I felt entrapped in the power of his notes for its melodious tune. It was so mesmerizing. From that day, I started paying keen attention to him. I had always wanted to know why he was so rude to everyone; why didn't he seem to be happy and participated in interacting with others around who were sincerely attempting to connect him; why didn't he feel comfortable even once when he was spending time with me; why did he leave an impression that he was not enjoying his life; why did he not seem to be interested in finding love of his life; why didn't he has special feelings for someone; all these unanswered questions were actually choking my mind. But I diverted my attention to the good time I spent with him.

He was so unpredictable. I never felt to be in the company of a normal person with whom I could think of spending a quality time. There was something he was trying to hide but I could never muster courage to ask him what it was.

I wanted to be in his arms forever. I wanted him to be my pillow, so that I could hug him every night. I wanted to be his only love. I wanted to carve a special place in his heart; a shadow who was following him all the time.

Indirectly I was trying to share my earnest feelings for him. But suddenly he got an important call. He got miffed for a while. I didn't know whose call that was. His eyes were stood up broadly. That time he took out the other cell phone (wireless landline) from his pocket. He told me to excuse him as he had to attend an important meeting. All of it happened so suddenly that I couldn't ask him where he was going. After that episode in the night that followed I called him but only to know that his phone was switched off. I was nervous and thinking why he had switched off his mobile?

Next morning when I woke up, I received his reply on my phone.

> *"Hey Pallavi*
>
> *Sorry for yesterday's behavior. It was nothing serious. So no need to worry. I was just panic and had to go in hurry as I have got an important work.*

I need to go. I have to switch off my phone for few days and also we wouldn't be able to meet. Catch you later.

Take Care."

I got distressed; because I wouldn't able to meet him for next few days. But I felt better than yesterday at least he informed me. It was alright. There was nothing to worry about.

Koregaon Park...

I was feeling bored to death. Eesha was busy in her work. She had gone to attend a Seminar in the O hotel. I could not understand why she decided to attend such an uninteresting seminar. Sid was busy in his work. Aryan was out of reach since the day we had our first night walk in Koregaon Park. I tried to call him several times but he did not respond even once. Mom and dad had gone for their friend's anniversary party. I switched on the TV, I kept on surfing the channels, then I watched some songs, latest movie trailer, then I was watching Shin-Chan cartoon for some time. But I was soon tired as there was nothing to watch.

I switched on the news channel so that I would get some information what's was going around us. I went in the kitchen to make some coffee. I made a cup of coffee and returned to the hall. I was sipping a mouthful of coffee. I sat in the corner of our window. I found myself thinking about Aryan.

The breaking News flashed on TV.

"A bomb blast ripped near German bakery in Pune just few Minutes before. 17 people died and 60 people were injured."

I surfed several news channels to get more information. I was feeling so terrible and dull after knowing about the blast. The bomb blast shook up the entire city completely. Ripped apart the German Bakery resulted in extensive damage and killed 17 people. More than 45 people had been rushed to hospital with varying degrees of injury. The blast which took place at 7.15pm when the bakery was milling with people, many of them were foreigners

I switched off the TV and went into my room; I fell on bed but was stark awake. I didn't know when my mom and dad would return from party. Around midnight, my phone rang and I was trying hard to force open my eyes. I took my phone in one hand and I saw an unknown (landline) number flashing on the screen. I didn't respond as it was an unknown number. I put my mobile on silent mode and I slept. But it again vibrated within a minute and it was the same number again. I woke up and received the call.

Unknown number: Hello. Is this Pallavi speaking, a trek leader of MH-Trek Club?

Me: Yes I am speaking. Who are you?

Unknown number: I am calling you from Ruby Hall Clinic.

I found a person in recent bomb blast that ripped German Bakery. I don't know how this person is related to you or not.

I just found your card in the wallet. Please come fast and help us identify that person. It would help us too. I hope you understood.

I hung up the phone.

My mind wasn't functioning properly. I started thinking about my friends and other members of my club. Who might be this person? At that time of the hour I didn't know what to do. I called Eesha but her cell phone was switched off; she had a bad habit of switching off her cell phone in the night. After then, I called Aryan but his cell phone was too switched off.

Finally I called up Sid, he received my call and I told him everything. When I hung up the phone, I told my parents about the call that I had received from ruby hall clinic. I told them that I was going there with Sid. I told them that one of the trekker from my **TREK CLUB** had sustained injuries.

Dad: Okay beta, do inform us once you recognized that person. If you need anything call me and go safely.

Me: Okay dad.

I took the keys of my car and unlocked the door to get into the car, I drove so fast. I picked up Sid on the way. Unwanted tension was building up my mind. I asked Sid to call Eesha. He dialed; but still her cell phone was still switched off. I found myself shouting at Sid, repeatedly demanding why Eesha had switched off her cell phone. I called him an idiot. Meanwhile dad's call flashed on my cellphone's screen, I gestured Sid to receive the call as I was driving.

"Hello Uncle", Sid spoke.

Dad: Beta, did you reach at the hospital?

Sid: No Uncle.

I told Sid to put phone on speaker.

Me: Dad will you please call Eesha's parents and ask where she was. I called her but her mobile was switched off.

Dad: Okay.

Ruby Hall Clinic

After talking with my dad, Sid put my mobile over the dash board, after some minutes we reached at the hospital. We got down from car and ran towards hospital. There was so much rush in the hospital. I asked at the reception counter. I'm Pallavi MH-TREK club leader, I got call from here.

Receptionist: Yes. Go straight and take first left, you will find Dr. Mehra there. Talk with her.

We ran from there, I found Dr. Mehra there but she was surrounded by many people were talking to her, I tried to go there and talked, but there was so much rush. I was feeling restless, so finally I managed to find my way through the crowd and begged for Dr. Mehra's attention.

Me: I'm Pallavi I got call from here before sometime.

SAMRUDDHI PEDGAONKAR; NIKHIL SALUNKE

Dr. Mehra: Yes. Just give me few minutes.

Dr. Mehra was looking like an assertive person, who must be turning 40. Her short light brown hair was remarkable spot of her beauty; she wore an *apron* and a stethoscope hanged around her shoulders.

Dr. Mehra: Pallavi, come with me; in the ICU section. But you have to wear gloves and mask; without wearing those no one was allowed inside.

Burnt patient is a trauma patient. We wore those protecting gears. Doctor opened the ICU door and we went inside the ward; there were six to seven beds in a row. But to make divisions there were one curtain in between two beds.

When I entered inside, many thoughts crowded my mind, as we went on after setting eyes on those persons lying on the beds attached with scores of medical equipment continually monitoring vital parameters, I felt dizzy. Many of them were so badly disheveled that no one could have recognized them. I didn't watch them properly but while walking with doctor I could saw only little. We were standing near the last bed.

Doctor asked us to take a closer look at the person. We went closer; how could we not recognize her? I looked at Sid only to know that eyes were transfixed at me. Our jaws dropped. Right half part of the person's body was badly burnt, right from the cheeks to the upper portion which joins the shoulder part.

Me: Yes. We know.

Doctor left from there.

We both were shell shocked; were unable to digest what we just saw, the burnt person lying on a bed. Sid's phone rang and he handed over his cell to me. It was my dad. I came outside the ICU to receive the call.

Me: Hello, Dad Pallavi here.

Dad: Beta, why are you not receiving my calls? We called Eesha's parents but they also don't know where she was? And I told them about bomb blast.

Me: I forgot my phone in the car. Dad, listen. I found Eesha here in the hospital. Please come to the hospital with Eesha's parents.

At that time, I lost a sense of everything around. I was consoling myself; I was trying to give false assurance to myself that the person lying on the bed might not be Eesha. My eyes were brimmed with tears unknowingly and I plonked on the bench. After few minutes, I realized that Sid was inside. I went inside, Sid was standing still. I was staring at Eesha. How? When? Why? These questions were repeatedly bothering me and there was no chance of finding answers to them.

I looked at Sid's he was still very shocked. Sid didn't accept that Eesha was injured in bomb blast. I started crying. I was unable to stop my tears. I could not believe that she was Eesha. How could she? I was totally blank. Sid didn't move from there. I move an inch towards him and I put my hand on his shoulder. Sid was frozen and did not respond. I was talking to Sid. But he screamed.

Sid: Look Pallavi, she isn't our Eesha. No. She is not. I know she must be some other girl who resembles Eesha. Nothing bad can happen to our Eesha. Nobody can do like this to our Eesha. You know she didn't trouble anyone. She is such a sweet girl. She is the first one to help other people. Then how can she lie on hospital bed.

He was not in a condition to listen. Finally Sid broke down with deep sobs and hugged me. It was very difficult for me to see Eesha like this. I came outside along with Sid and sat on bench.

Nurse came and told us to complete the procedure of surgery. We both were staring at each other.

Nurse: Yes, we have to do surgery.

Meanwhile Dr. Mehra came.

Dr. Mehra: Pallavi, she is in a very critical condition so we have to perform surgery immediately. She was thermally injured. So surgery is a must. Due to the high temperature generated after the blast, her upper layer of skin burnt; there is a severe damage to her skin's tissue so it's essential to perform surgery. And we have to immediately go for steam inhalation because the smoke emanated soon after the blast has entered her lungs. It would be difficult for her to take breath. She has lost much of her blood so nothing can be said right now.

Me: doctor can you please explain about thermal injury?

Doctor: Pallavi when a person is in direct contact with flames a hot surface or fire, he suffers from thermal injury.

Me: Okay doctor.

Doctor: Don't worry, Pallavi. I will update you time to time.. Did you call her parents?

Me: Yes.

Doctor: Okay, then we will shift her to the operation theater; you go with nurse and complete the procedure.

Dr. Mehra put her hand on my shoulder and she left.

Nurse came after 5-10 minutes and she took me at the counter to complete the procedure. That time I realized that I was not carrying any money with me nor did I carry ATM cards. I came here without carrying my wallet. So I looked at Sid but he was not mentally stable. I didn't call him. I forgot my mobile in car. But I remembered that Sid's mobile was with me. So I called dad but his mobile was out of range. So I started to fill the form.

While I was completing or filling the information mine and Eesha's parents came. I first I looked at my dad; he came near me with Eesha's dad.

Me: dad I called you but your cell phone was out of range. Before submitting this form we have to pay and I don't have money.

Dad: Okay, we will look at this you go. Don't worry beta.

Eesha's mom was not in a condition to listen anything. She was crying a lot. She wants to see Eesha but Doctor already shifted her to Operation Theater. I called dad and I hugged him so tightly. While he was busy with the procedure. Dad was consoling me. Dad put his hand on my head and told me to be strong. Nothing can go wrong. Go talk to Sid.

Then Eesha's dad and my dad were completing the remaining procedure. My mom was with Eesha's mom; my mom's eyes were also filled with tears. But she was consoling Eesha's mom. I was sitting near Sid. We all were not in a condition to talk with each other. We were still in the dark about what was going on. We were unsure about what doctor would tell us. It was a difficult situation for everybody but particularly for Eesha's parents. She was only child of her parents. If they lost her then for their life would be shattered.

She was my best friend I know, Even a slightest thought that something can go wrong with her made me frightened. I was totally blank and certainly not ready to accept these things. I could not even imagine the condition of Eesha's parents.

Then Nurse came and returned me Eesha's belongings that they had found at the site of the bomb blast. At that time Eesha's mom walked towards me and I handed over Eesha's belongings to her. Sid also looked at them, her half burnt wallet, scarf, and her burnt college ID card. Sid had gifted that scarf to Eesha. I still remember that scarf. Eesha loved to wear scarf. Sid stood up from the bench and took the scarf from aunty's hand. Eesha's mom couldn't control herself. My mom was consoling Eesha's mom. When I saw Eesha's stuff I ran outside, I cried uncontrollably. I was literally trembling while crying. As I sat outside, my shudders did not stop, no matter how much I tried but I could not help myself from sobbing…

Sid came and sat beside me. We both didn't utter a single word and were staring in nothingness. Everyone was tense. Negative thoughts were crowding my mind; I could not stop thinking that if we lose Eesha forever then…

Me: What happened to her? How come she caught in this? Sid I'm so much scared for Eesha? Will she be fine or?

Sid: She has to live for us and she will be fine Pallavi don't worry.

We all were facing such situation for the first time. We were hoping that she will be fine after surgery.

Both came inside where Eesha's surgery was going on. Eesha's mom was sitting like a statue. We were all waiting for Eesha's surgery to get over. What will happen? What will be the situation? What doctor will say? All questions were running in my mind.

I looked at Sid he was completely broken into pieces. Dad was also consoling Eesha's father. He too was shattered after saw Eesha's belongings. They weren't screaming. I sat next to Sid. I put my hand on Sid's shoulder and told him that everything will be alright. We didn't utter a word. Almost five hours passed but there was no sign of doctor to emerge out from Operation Theater. We were all eagerly waiting for Doctors and had held our breath thinking what doctor would tell us? How was Eesha?

Finally doctor came outside with her surgery team. Sid got up immediately and moved towards her. Then we all gathered there. He asked her, *"Doctor how she is feeling now?"*

Dr. Mehra: She is okay. Not to worry. But her right upper side of body is half burnt and little bit part of her face. And she

SAMRUDDHI PEDGAONKAR; NIKHIL SALUNKE

got some marks on right side of her forehead. Her skin is so sensitive that it will take time for her to recover or her wounds to get healed. She will be under observation till she responds properly. Eesha has lost so much blood in her body.

As I said earlier that her skin was so sensitive and that was the reason for deeper injury. First layer of her skin or cell and tissue burned so the road to recovery for difficult for her. She would feel so weak for some days. Because there was so much loss of blood, her skin was looking more reddish which will change the shed which might be also visible for some days. Doctors informed us that we could see her only after wearing hand gloves, apron & mask, if you want to go near her. Doctors told us that such precaution was necessary for patient & those who come to meet them.

She was sleeping. I was hoping that after 24 hours she would start responding slowly. Till then we had to wait. One most important thing, Doctors told us to give her emotional support when she would respond or when she would open her eyes. They told us to put a smile on our faces as we went near her. Doctor Mehra warned us to avoid any questions related to bomb blast. She told us that asking her that why she went there might impact her mentally. She was lucky that she hadn't lost any part of her body. Doctors told us that her left side was burnt so they asked us to try our best to console ourselves and to her too. They said that burn patient was a trauma patient. So they asked us to take care. Dr Mehra assured us that she would update us from time to time about her sittings and surgeries in future.

Eesha's Dad: More surgery?

Dr.Mehra: Yes sir! Till the wounds get dry. There is so much heat still in the skin so we have to do it. We will take sittings. Now let's see how she responds, but sittings are compulsory. And after then we will decide about the cosmetic surgery.

Dr Mehra: All of you support her mentally. I am saying this again and again because there are so many cases we had seen that people lost their mental stability in such incidences. Patients then start questioning themselves that How people would look at them. Now I am not looking good like others. Nobody will accept me etc.

So I am sure you would support her mentally and boost her confidence. It will take some more time but till then you don't lose your confidence. Especially girls are so emotional, so please be strong and try your best. And special instructions - only one or two persons will go in the room at a time, not more than that.

Eesha's mom asked Dr. Mehra that whether they could go inside to see their daughter right now. Dr. Mehra agreed but told Eesha's mom to control her emotions and instructed nurse to provide a hospital clothes to everyone. When Eesha' mom entered the room Eesha was sleeping.

Eesha's mom sat near Eesha and put her hand on Eesha's forehead. On the right hand side there was saline attached. Her body was fully covered, only her face was visible. There was oxygen mask on her face. Eesha's mom started crying and said that she didn't want to see Eesha in this condition. We all consoled her and tried to stop her crying. Eesha's dad stood near Eesha's mom and he was staring at her daughter. He was also broken. He was in a fix whether to vent out himself or to handle his wife. I found that Sid was not inside the room. So I came outside the room. I saw him. He was still sitting on the bench and crying.

Me: What are you doing here Sid? Come inside to see her. Let's go.

Sid: I can't see her like this; I don't have guts to see her. I can't come. You go.

Me: Come on Sid. You are so strong and can control yourself. No need to worry. She will be fine. Just come for sake of her.

Sid: no I will not, it's not possible for me.

I held his hand and forced him to come inside. We went inside. Sid couldn't control his tears. He went outside. I followed him and put my hand on his shoulder. Sid hugged me very tightly and cried a lot. My mom also started crying after she saw Eesha. Dad was trying to keep her calm and quiet. My mom-dad told Eesha's parents to stay there.

My dad took Eesha's dad aside and said, "We will come tomorrow. Take care of yourself and Eesha will be fine soon. If you need anything just call me I will be there in a minute. Don't worry too much. Everything will be alright."

My mom-dad came towards me they told me to come after dropping Sid at his home. I nodded in yes. Sid was looking Eesha through the glass. He was so quiet. He didn't utter a single word. I told Eesha's parents to take care of themselves and informed them that I would be there in the morning. I grabbed his hand and we got in the car. I was driving.

Suddenly Sid said, *"Why it happened with her?"* He was crying and was totally broken inside. I consoled him.

Me: Come on Sid. She will be fine very soon. Now it's our duty to help to make her fine as soon as possible. We will help her to feel normal. We won't let her feel bad for whatever happened to her. We will make her strong. But for that we have to be normal and strong from now. She is so lucky, Sid, that she is alive. There are so many people who have lost their loved ones. Sid nodded. But still he was heartbroken. I dropped him at his place. I got down from the car. I hugged him very tightly and held him for long to make him feel better. But it didn't work. A tear dropped down from my left eye. I wiped it. I consoled myself. I had to stop myself. I had decided that I will take care of both Eesha and Sid. I got into my car and turned to leave for my home. Dad opened the door. They were still awake.

Dad: Beta, are you okay? And how is Sid now? Is he fine?

Me: Yes, Dad I am okay now. Don't' worry. And Sid will be fine.

Dad: Okay. Now you go and take a sleep. Tomorrow we have to go to hospital.

Me: Yes dad. Good night. You both too take care. I get in my room and slept on my bed. Many thoughts were coming in my mind about Eesha, our friendship, how we meet first time, everything was flashing in front of me. How we did enjoy, studies. While recollecting memories suddenly a thought about Aryan came in my mind. I called him but his phone was also switch off. I tried again three times afterwards but still his cellphone was switched off. I was still unable to come to

111

terms with the fact that really it did happen with Eesha. I was trying to sleep but whole night I couldn't sleep. Whole night I was thinking about Eesha. I was crying a lot.

In the morning, I got ready to go hospital. My phone was ringing. Sid called me.

Sid: Pallavi you come directly to the hospital. I have already reached.

Me: Yeah, that's fine.

Destroyed German Bakery

When I started my moped and was on the way to hospital; a thought of visiting German Bakery. I turned my moped to that direction. I parked my moped near Osho Garden and walked towards German Bakery.

With me; there were bystanders who were looking at the destroyed German Bakery after bomb blast. The entire area was cordoned off by police. Several policemen were collecting evidence from the remains of the bakery. Two policemen and press reporters were talking to each other. And I was thinking how blast must have taken place.

The blast site that shook the cultural city of Maharashtra state had turned into tourist destination with many people thronging in to catch the glimpses of what was once a bakery thriving with people. This explosion has highlighted the fact that erstwhile pensioner's paradise too was unsafe like many other metro cities of India. Panic gripped the city as the news of the blast spread.

The entire city was under darkness. The blast had left bakery into a heap of debris; dozens of people died in the blast including foreigners. Many recounted that how body parts of some of the dead ones were strewn on the North Main road and the lane adjacent to The O Hotel. The reports of the devastation were still coming in and the numbers of people killed, injured and affected by this blast were continually changing as some of injured succumbed to their injuries. I couldn't bear to wait there, the devastation and the gloom that followed made me impossible to stand near the bakery.

I went to the hospital. Uncle was sitting outside on the bench. They were in a sleepy mood. Aunty was inside with Eesha. Aunty was half slept still held Eesha's Hand. I went inside and woke up aunty.

Aunty: Beta when did you came?

Me: Yes, aunty. Just a few minutes ago.

We all came outside the room. Sid woke up uncle. We told them to go home to take some rest. And we told them to come in the evening. We told them not to worry as I & Sid were there to take care of Eesha. Eesha's mom-dad hadn't slept in the night. They were feeling restless. I forced them to go.

Eesha was sleeping. She was still unconscious. There was still few hours left to clock 24 hours. For some time me and Sid both sat outside. I sensed that Sid was still feeling scared and was thinking a lot about Eesha. I walked towards coffee machine and took two cups of coffee. I know it will help to calm our minds. When I came with two cups of coffee, Sid wasn't there on bench. The bench was empty. For some seconds I looked here and there. Then I opened Eesha's room's door. There I found Sid was sitting near Eesha.

He took her left hand in his hand. Sid was looking at her burnt part. It was still in red and brown shades. Her face was and her only left hand was open. There was saline on that hand. Whole body was packed. He wanted to touch her but he couldn't. His fingers were shivering. He had taken her hand and he kissed her hand so softly. He was holding her left hand. I have never seen him in emotional state of mind. First time he was totally broken, not uttering a word, not even asking questions. I always remembered him to be someone cool, naughty and flirt. That day Sid was completely opposite. He kissed her forehead and put her hand down slowly on bed. Sid was crying a lot, he was trying to stop but he could not control himself. I was still standing there and observing Sid. Sid saw me and I call him outside. He came outside and I wiped all his tears.

I handed over one cup of coffee to Sid. We sat on the bench and drinking coffee. We sat quietly for some time. We both didn't utter a single word.

Sid: "I know Pallavi, sometimes I didn't listen to her. I flirted with other girls but still she never complained. I frequently went for parties but she never stopped me. I teased her lot frequently addressed her as a Persian cat just to notice her reaction. I loved to watch her get angry at me. I simply denied accompanying both of you even after she insisted to accompany you for shopping. But now I promise her that I will do everything for her. She has to tell me whatever she wants. I will go with her wherever she feels each time she asks me to come and at any time. I won't leave her alone even for fraction of seconds.

I will help her to be her normal self again. She will again look beautiful for me. I will be always with her. She will be alright. I know these things have given her so much pain. I am unable to see her like this. And I bet you will take care of her much more than me. I want her to smile. I want her love. I want to see her happy. Eesha I am sorry. If I was there, I wouldn't have let these happen with her. If I was there I could have saved her. Sorry Eesha I'm so really sorry. I love you."

While talking about Eesha Sid's eyes were filled with tears. He was feeling Eesha's pain. He was feeling so guilty and blaming himself. Sid burst into tears so hard that it was impossible to tell him to control himself. My eyes too filled with tears. Why it happened to her? I knew that these wounds gave her lot of pain. When doctor pricked her injection, when the saline needle was put in her skin, we could feel the pain. When the bomb blast exploded, the flames gave her so much pain, how much blood she must have lost from her body.

I told him, *"Sid It didn't happen because of you. So stop blaming yourself. Neither was it Eesha's mistake. It's already written in her destiny. And now we are with her so don't worry."*

Sid put his head on my shoulder and cried a lot and while consoling him I too started crying.

Me: Sid we will make her better, we will take care of her. We will be always with her.

In the hope of...

After some time we came inside. Eesha's mom and dad came after post lunch. I was slept on bench. They woke me up. I stood up and gave a seat to aunty. Sid and uncle were sitting outside. Dr. Mehra came for her check up. 24 hours were over. After so many hours Eesha was trying to open her eyes. Everyone stood beside Eesha.

Dr. Mehra: Yes Eesha. Try to open your eyes slowly. Nurse was opening the covered part of the Eesha's body. Nurse put the covered glass part at the corner of the room. Still her body covered with white color bed sheet. And doctor was checking her heart rate, pulses. Eesha tried her best to open her eyes slowly. I had crossed my fingers and I was praying. I could feel goose bumps on my whole body.

She opened her eyes. She was watching everyone and was looking everywhere. As if she didn't know where was she? She was watching saline on her left hand. Doctor was still checking her. Then she saw her right hand. She was so confused. Then doctor asked her how she was feeling. She didn't give any response to doctor. She was trying to move her fingers slowly but they were paining a lot. She didn't smile.

She glanced at every one of us. After some minutes, she asked doctor what had happened to her. I guessed she knew that what happened with her but she wanted to listen it from doctor. Dr. Mehra told her everything.

Dr. Mehra: "Eesha, you were found in bomb blast that occurred two days before German Bakery. You were admitted here for more than 24 hours. Unfortunately your upper left side of the body got little bit burnt in bomb blast."

Eesha looked at her right hand. The feeling wasn't digestible. She looked at her mom and dad. She turned her neck on right side and her eyes filled with tears. Tears were rolling out of her eyes and streaming down her cheeks. Eesha's mom came near her and she wiped her tears with the napkin. Doctor came near Eesha and consoled her.

Dr. Mehra: "Look Eesha. Don't cry. It will give you more pain. Stop crying first. And you are a very brave girl. You have fought with the bomb blast. You fought while we were doing surgery. You know Eesha you are so lucky that you have got another life to live. You have got one more chance to live. You are saved from bomb blast. There are so many people who had lost their life, children, their parents, grandparents. Many people had lost their love one. You are so lucky Eesha. And don't underestimate yourself dear, we all are with you. You will be fine soon. Cause you are so strong girl and brave girl.

Eesha were staring at doctor. And doctor said to her, yes, you can trust me."

When Dr. Mehra was leaving the room, she told us to give her juice, coconut water etc. Dr. Mehra excused Eesha's dad so he went outside with doctor and I also went.

Dr Mehra: Sir, now Eesha is conscious so we have to do steam inhalation process. Eesha's dad asked her the details of this procedure.

Dr. Mehra: We have to clear her lungs as the smoke of the bomb blast got inside her body. So we have to perform this procedure.

Eesha's Dad: Will it cause her further pain to Eesha? And how will you do it?

Dr. Mehra: It won't cause much of pain to Eesha, and we will do it through pipe, and we will adjust the pressure. So don't worry sir she will feel good after that and it will take hardly 6-7 minutes. So we can remove the oxygen mask. We will do it within half an hour.

After half an hour Eesha had gone through the process. When process got over we went inside the ward and Eesha's oxygen mask was removed.

Me: Eesha how are you feeling now? Did it hurt you?

Eesha: I'm feeling good and expecting that pain will soon vanish ASAP.

Doctor gave the list of tablets, syrups and cream. Aunty and uncle sat near Eesha and they were consoling her. She was not in a mental condition to accept this.

I & Sid were waiting outside. Eesha wasn't ready to believe. When aunty uncle came outside, I and Sid went inside the room. She was looking at me and then glanced at Sid. Her eyes filled with tears. I wanted to go and hug her but I couldn't. We both went near her bed and we sat near her.

Eesha was trying to hold Sid's hand but suddenly Sid held her hand and I put my hand on her head. She burst into tears then. She was crying a lot. I wiped Eesha's tears and consoled her. We told her to be strong and that everything would be alright.

Eesha: Why me, Pallavi?

I couldn't answer these questions. I couldn't imagine what she was feeling that time. She was looking so different.

Both aunty and uncle went to buy juice. Then they came with a glass of watermelon juice. And suddenly uncle left to buy tablets and injection and cream. Aunty sat near Eesha on that chair.

Aunty: Eesha lets drink this juice now. You love watermelon, so I got watermelon juice for you.

Eesha wasn't ready to give response. Eesha cried a lot in front of aunty. Aunty didn't speak single word and she also started crying. She put her hand on Eesha's head. After sometime aunty made her agree to drink juice. So we helped Eesha to sit properly. Then aunty was feeding her juice. Aunty held the glass and she was drinking juice by straw. Everything was going normal. After sometime I called Dada that Eesha had opened her eyes and she was feeling good now. Dad told me that he along with my mother would come to meet Eesha. I said ok.

Mom and dad came to meet Eesha talked with her, talked with her parents and they went to home.

On that night, we told Eesha's parents to go home to take rest. I and Sid stayed there. Sid was trying to crack some jokes so that Eesha could feel good. And she felt much better. I sensed that. I was feeling so happy after observing that slowly Eesha was returning to normalcy. I felt that she was feeling normal or feeling happy. But she needed assistance to carry out routine activities. She depended heavily on us. She could not even brush her teeth by herself. So Sid or I helped her to brush her teeth. She didn't even hold the glass of water by herself.

I held her arm and helped her to sit and then first time I combed Eesha's hair. She was admitted to hospital. It was all messed up. It was not easy to comb her hair. Eesha was shouting when I was combing her hair. I could sense that it was giving her pain. Then I tied her hair. I cleaned her face by wet tissue; it helped her to feel little bit fresh. It was very difficult for us and for her also. So many times Eesha were staring at her wounds, continually noticing her skin. I softly warned her not to stare at her wounds. But she could not stop herself. While staring the wounds her eyes automatically filled with tears. I understood her. She was not much talking. I knew that she was not in a mental condition to talk.

Later after feeding her coconut water we felt asleep. I was on another bed and Sid was slept on chair. Eesha was still in sleep. So after sometime doctor came for checkup. And doctor told us that tomorrow morning they would do first sitting. So I asked doctor that what would be done in the first sitting.

A frightening dream...

Almost one week passed. It was a shocking morning for us. I told Sid to bring coffee for us. He went. I was sitting there with Eesha. She already slept. I was reading a newspaper. Sid came with two cups of hot coffee. We were discussing the news published in that day's newspaper. Timetable for HSC examination was published in the newspaper. Suddenly a thought touched our mind of our own exams. I wished that Eesha should recover as soon as possible before our final exam begins. So that she could give her exams well. While we were discussing this suddenly Eesha started screaming loudly. She was shouting,

"Please help! Help! Please save him."

She woke up with scary expressions on her face. We shuddered. We sat beside her and tried to control her. But she didn't talk so much. Neither had we asked her who was, she trying to save. I gave her a glass of water. She drank it. I rang a bell and nurse came for checkup. I would call a doctor she would be there. After some time, then doctor came to ask.

Dr. Mehra: Eesha how are you feeling today?

Eesha answered, *"I am a bit better doctor. I just had a nightmare so screamed. Nothing much."*

Dr. Mehra: Okay. Now you have to start eating light food from tomorrow. And now from tomorrow we will only apply a cotton bandage on your burnt part and wounds. So that you can try to move your hand on your own and soon you will be all right too.

Eesha: Ok doctor. It's good news for me. Thank you.

Dr. Mehra: Don't say thanks to me. It's my duty. But your friends have saved you dear. They spent days and nights here to take care of you. They even took care of your parents. You're so lucky to have such a good friends like them.

When Dr. Mehra went outside I followed them and excused her.

Me: Doctor, I want to talk you about Eesha.

Dr. Mehra: Yes Pallavi. I am listening.

Me: Doctor is it possible to do plastic surgery on her left part of Burnt body?

Dr. Mehra: No Pallavi. It's not possible now. Because Eesha's skin is so sensitive and it will take several months to recover those wounds. This is not the right time. And yes plastic surgery is possible, but not now. This option can be considered after a year.

Don't worry I will suggest you. But before that the most important thing is that please make sure that you will give attention to Eesha. She needs you now. You know how emotional girls are. Her behavior is changing. Every day she is responding very well. She is laughing but she is deeply hurt. And I know she is feeling too much pain inside. So please do understand her and talk with her as much as you can.

Me: Doctor. Eesha had a nightmare some time before. She was shouting words like blood and save his life. That's why I pressed the bell to call you.

Dr. Mehra: Yeah. It's okay. I guess maybe she had remembered the events at the time of bomb blast. She had a night mare of it. No need to worry. It happens. As I said talk to her as much as you can, she will feel good. I came inside after talking with doctor.

Sid asked me what doctor said? Did you tell them about her nightmare? I gestured him with hands indicating that I would tell him later. Then I asked Eesha what she wanted to eat?

Eesha: Today, I want to eat Roti & Paneer ki sabji.

Me: Ok fine. I and Sid would bring your favorite *Paneer Patiala* and *rotis*. Till then take rest.

We requested doctor to bring the outside food for her concern. Doctor agreed but warned us not to bring again.

Seeing Unseen...

While I was about to start disclosing about Eesha, I grabbed Rohan's hand very tightly. My eyes were full of tears while narrating him how I it was painful to see Eesha in pain, I have seen Eesha's eyes at that time. He gave me a glass of water. When I drank I realized that I held Rohan's hand. I left his hand instantly and said sorry to him and begun to tell him.

First nurse came for dressing Eesha's burn part and wounds. She came with big trolley of bandages, two long tubes of cream and cotton and in one container there is water and there was sponge and Dettol bottle. I and Sid were watching at trolley. Then she told Sid please go outside, he said yes. I sought permission from nurse to stay inside as she did her dressing. I offered to help her. She gave me a smile and allowed me inside. And she closed the door.

126

Nurse told me we to turn Eesha on right side so that she could start. She wanted to complete the back part first. For that we had to open her gown. Slowly I turned Eesha on right side. I tried my best not to hurt her. Eesha put her right hand far from her body. I opened all the knots of the gown she had worn. Then nurse took the sponge and dipped into water. She put some anti-infectant in that sponge and started cleaning Eesha's back. After cleaning her back nurse took towel and started dabbing her back dry.

I was tensed as it will not hurt her. I was blank. Nurse told me to turn her straight and I turned Eesha straight. This time she got hurt while moving and tried to control her pain. Eesha was sleeping straight. Nurse opened Eesha's front knot of the gown and suddenly I turned my head in opposite direction and I closed my eyes. I held corner of the bed very tightly. I didn't have courage to open my eyes for fraction of seconds.

But I opened my eyes and saw Eesha first. She was continuously staring at her body. She didn't even close her eyes for a second. I saw her body from so near. Almost half of her left side was burnt. Skin was looking like crushed paper. Her original skin was replaced with dark brown colored skin. From her shoulder towards her left breast and her left part of torso, all was trampled down. There were blood clots formed on burnt part of her body. Eesha was suffering from terrible paining nurse was cleaning and dressing her wound. Her facial expressions were enough to know that how much she suffered. But she didn't utter a single word nor did she make a slight noise. Her eyes filled with tears.

Nurse put ointment on her wounds and she wrapped a bandage on that. She tied all the knots and put blanket to cover her whole body. She told Eesha that she was so brave. You didn't even make noise.. She opened the door and left the room. I turned and glanced at Eesha. I was shocked to glance at her.

When I had seen in Eesha's eyes we both had tears in our eyes. There was sorrow & pain in those tears. I was helpless as I could only hold her hand in mine. I couldn't hug her how much I wanted to. We both wanted to hug her so tightly. But we couldn't. I had apologized Eesha and my tears were falling. I couldn't control myself.

Sid came inside but he couldn't know why we both were crying. Suddenly I ran from there. I couldn't control myself. Sid glanced at Eesha as if he wanted to ask her but she too was crying hard. He came outside the ward to ask me. I hugged him and yelled.

Me: Sid, today I saw Eesha's left burnt part. Why this happened with Eesha? Tell me Sid. I don't want to see her in this situation.

Sid: Pallavi, if you are crying like this then who will support Eesha? Who will console her? Only you can. Now stop crying. You told me that we will control our emotions; pain and what are you doing? Come on wipe your tears now and be strong.

Me: But Sid I can't.

Sid: No Pallavi. You have to. We don't have an option until Eesha recovers.

I wiped my tears and I saw Sid's eyes were filled with tears too. We both went inside near to Eesha. I put my head on Eesha's right shoulder and Sid took her hand on his. I saw he held her hand very tightly. Eesha started blaming herself.

"Why I went there? If I wouldn't have gone there, then this wouldn't have happened with me. Now everyone will look at me whenever I shall be passing from road. They will feel guilt while looking at my half burnt body. Now onwards I have to wear full clothes. I couldn't wear bangles, accessories. You know Pallavi I love to wear all those things. I always loved to go shopping for them with you. Now I couldn't even go for shopping. I won't look like before, hot and beautiful."

She was pretending herself to be normal. But her eyes were telling the truth. I wiped her tears.

Then within some minutes nurse came with the food. We got a chance to change our mood. I took it from nurse. I gave it to Sid and teased him to feed her properly. He sat on the bed beside Eesha a little closer to her. Sid started feeding her but she refused to eat. Sid again took another one and fed her. But she refused again. She did it 4 to 5 times but Sid didn't stop feeding her nor did he get angry on her. Then at last she ate it. After finishing her lunch I told Eesha to take rest. I gave her some tablets which were kept on a table and glass of water. Eesha told me that those tablets are bitter in taste. I don't want to take this. We laughed at her. She too joined us.

After some time in the evening Eesha's parents came. I was slept on the chair. Aunty and uncle were happy to see Eesha in better condition than previous. Aunty woke me up.

I informed them, "she had her lunch well and she took her tablets too. Dr. Mehra will come soon. The nurse has told us that Dr. Mehra will come in the night for checkup. Today they will tell you everything. There are major chances to Eesha to get discharge in next week. Let's see what happens?"

Dr. Mehra came at around 9-9.30p.m. She greeted us and went inside. No one was inside except Dr. Mehra and Eesha.

Dr. Mehra didn't come till 45minutes. We were tensed and waiting for them. Many questions were running in my mind.

After they came there was a smile on their face. And I saw a hope in that smile. Dr. Mehra told us that Eesha was responding well to her medicines and she was mentally stable now. Tomorrow we would remove her both saline and cotton dressing.

After listening to this we all felt happy especially Eesha's parents. So after two days her saline was removed. She had kept under observation for one day. Her movement wasn't still restricted. But Eesha had night mare again. We were waiting to get her discharged from hospital. Next morning she got discharged. We took her home. In car I and Sid were sitting beside her. She was in the middle. Eesha's parents were sitting in front two seats. And Eesha's dad was driving and she held our hands. She was feeling excited to go home after a long time. Eesha came home after almost long time. I and Sid had decided to live at Eesha's home until she recovered completely and became independent like before. While entering into home Eesha needed some support. She didn't walk by herself. Doctors had prescribed strict diet for her. We teased her lot as she was unable to eat street food until she recovered.

I wanted to inform Aryan but his phone was still switched off. I was deeply worried but my mind was diverted in taking care of Eesha. I started missing him like a hell.

Eesha was looking pale as she lost her weight. The tablets and medicines had made her lose appetite. After one month our exams were going to start. I & Sid studied at Eesha's home in front of her. So that she would not feel alone and we could do our study. We wanted to be with her to take care of her. I was cleaning Eesha's body every day and applying cream after that. Sid's duty was feeding her food and after that I reminded her to take tablets. Doctor didn't give her permission to her to move left hand so much. She couldn't even walk by herself. Whenever she wanted to sit we gave her support. She was not ready to see her reflection in the mirror. She was avoiding and she was so scared to see herself in the mirror.

Sid was doing both things, his study and taking caring of Eesha. He spent so much time with Eesha hoping that she would recover fast. Sometimes I found her lost in thoughts that she often took time to respond. I knew Eesha was having nightmares. But she didn't speak about what exactly happened that night. How she faced that incidence? What did she saw that night?

Sometimes I found myself thinking about what she might be thinking. I knew one day she would share with Sid. So I didn't press her. Sid was doing everything for Eesha. He never complained. And I was sure that Eesha would be fine so soon because of him. I was waiting for that day when Eesha would walk by herself.

Our Exams...

We were doing our study so hard that we wanted to score high in finals. We both got placements; we both had cracked interviews so we had to score good in finals at any cost. But I observed that Sid wasn't studying properly. I asked him. He told me that he was feeling very bad for Eesha as she couldn't appear for her exams even if she had got placed. It was true that she had to drop in last year. I guessed Eesha heard conversation. A day after tomorrow she was feeling guilty as if everything had finished. We repeatedly asked her the reason for disappointment but she didn't disclose what was bothering her. We forced her to let us know. Finally she opened her mouth.

Eesha: You both are preparing for your exam but considering my condition I can't appear for the same. As soon as the result will be declared then you both will be occupied with your job and I shall be seating idle like this.

I and Sid looked at each other and we sensed that she might have heard our conversation. We tried to motivate Eesha in a positive manner.

Me: Eesha, whenever you will be fine like before then you can continue your final exams. And I am sure you will get good grades and better company than us.

Eesha: But Pallavi.

Me: Eesha. Think positively. Everything happens for a reason. So shed your negative thoughts.

Eesha: Ok. I can hope for the best.

Our exam was approaching. We were studying hard. Eesha was resting well and taking as much sleep as she could. One day prior to our exams was all set to begin Eesha fell down while trying to take tablets on her own. I & Sid both ran towards her. We helped her to get up and put her back to her bed. At that time I scolded her lot.

Eesha: You both were busy in your studies and tomorrow you have to go for exam so I didn't want to disturb you guys.

Sid was angry at her. But he didn't scold her. Instead of that he simply said.

Sid: Eesha you are our first priority. We don't want you to try something that will hurt you. Eesha you know we care a lot about you. Please don't do this again. You are very important for us. Please do take care of yourself.

Eesha: Hmm. Ok guys. I am sorry.

It was an unbeatable morning for us as our exam started. I & Sid were equally tensed.

Eesha: Guys. Best of luck and write well. I know you will do your best. And don't worry much I will be fine. I am waiting for you both to come.

Me & Sid: Yes Eesha. But you take care yourself for some time. We will be back soon.

Sid & Eesha were looking into each other. Sid went near her. He put his hand on her hand and said those three magical words. Eesha smiled at him. This time her smile was amazingly beautiful. There was a spark in her eyes too. Sid kissed on her forehead. And he asked her to take care.

We reached college. We were missing Eesha a lot. We reached in our classroom. My seat was on 4th bench in a first row and Sid got last bench in a 3rd row. We got papers and we started writing. For first half an hour I was writing curiously as there were some questions for which I had prepared well. In mid times when I was remembering the answer I looked at Sid to see how he is doing. Sid was writing carefully. At that time he looked at his right side row. There he found one bench empty. He remembered her. He looked at me. I gestured him to write well by blinking my eyes. When our exams got over I went near Sid. Paper was too good for both of us.

We left immediately from there and went to Eesha's home.

While going to her home I informed my mom-dad about paper. Eesha also asked us how our paper was and she felt good after listening that our paper was easy. It took almost 16 days to finish our exams. On our last paper everyone went for a party. But I & Sid didn't go. We went directly at Eesha's home. Later in the evening Sid returned to his home and he told me that he would join me on the next day afternoon at Eesha's home. I had already decided to stay at Eesha's home. Eesha was started walking slowly. But she still needed some support.

As we were busy in our preparations for examination, she had started using walking stick so that she could try walking on her own. She showed some improvement each day. I was so happy for her. One day at night, post dinner as we sat in the balcony.

Believing the unbelievable...

I was feeling so light that day. I wanted to spend that night while having endless talk with Eesha just by sitting beside her.

Me: Eesha how are you feeling now? Do you still feel pain while walking?

Eesha: Nope. Not that much as you would imagine.

I found Eesha was feeling low. She was avoiding an eye contact while talking with me. I finally asked her what was bothering her and she started talking to me only after ensuring that no one was around.

Eesha: Nothing. I remembered something that I wanted to tell you. But I don't understand from where I should start. I wanted to tell you since last few weeks but I kept quiet because of your exams.

Me: Eesha what are you talking about. I am not getting you. Please tell me whatever it is. I am confused. Eesha started narrating me.

"That day, when I went to O hotel to attend a seminar. You both refused to come but I went ahead. I took your moped and went. I didn't inform you that I was going there. I did not even inform Sid. It was pleasant experience for me. When it got over I came outside. I was happy. I had parked your moped in the lane between hotel and the bakery. I came and took out a scarf from moped's storage box. While tying scarf on my face, I saw something but I was confused so I stepped towards it. I reached the main road. I was waiting for the car to stop so that I can take turn to go. While I was waiting, I saw him little bit. I didn't recognize him at the first sight.

I was trying to recognize him. He had a beard. When I recognized I thought of going near to him. But within fraction of second a bomb exploded. I was thrown away from bakery. After few minutes as I was trying to sit and get up but, I was trying to open my eyes but eyes were burning. I could open them only little bit. Due to loud thud of bomb blast, I could not hear anything. Everything around was blurred, I was losing my vision after coming in contact with flames and smoke everywhere. My eyes were half opened but I had lost my vision. After some time I regained my sense. I realized that I was alive. There were some bodies lied on the floor pouring blood from it."

She added, "I didn't know that my left side was burnt. I didn't feel my left hand for fraction of seconds. I lay in a pool of blood. But my body was paining. Some children were spread there. They had died. In front of me there was someone's hand had dropped down. There was so much ash that I was unable to see clearly. So many people had died there on the spot. Some were injured. Some people might have lost their children. Few had lost their hands and legs. I saw blood was flowing from bodies. There was utter chaos and fire engine's bell could be heard from a distance. When I saw them I shouted twice and pleaded them to save him. Save him. I was trying to locate him. But I had lost my vision. I fell there unconscious. I didn't found him even after searching for him for past few minutes. I didn't find him. But I guess. It was my nightmare. I remember shouting for him in the hospital too."

Me: Eesha, control yourself. Don't cry. Eesha who was he? The guy you were trying to recognize. Why were you shouting for him? Do you remember him? What might have happened to him?

Eesha: Yes. But I am not sure.

Me: Who was he?

Eesha: I guess he was Aryan. I'm not sure about him. I couldn't recognize him properly.

After listening to Eesha I insisted her to take his name again. She repeated again. Shocked, I put hand on my mouth. My heart started beating fast. My eyes grew big. I felt shiver in my body. Many unanswered question arose in my mind. I found the answer to the question that why his mobile was switched off. That's why he didn't contact me for past two months. Is he ok? Is he alive or dead? So many negative thoughts were running in my mind. I took out my cell phone from my bag and I call him again. I called him thrice. I was scared. I had lost control. I started crying. My hand was shivering while punching his phone number. I was clueless; I did not know what to do? How will I get to know about him?

Eesha wasn't getting anything. She was repeatedly asking me that why I was reacting so much. My mind was losing control.

I screamed, *"Because I love him damn it."*

Eesha was shocked. She didn't know this. Neither had I told anyone as I myself wasn't sure about my feelings for him.

Me: Eesha, for god sake please say that he wasn't Aryan.

I plonked down. I was asking her how I could find him. I was asking myself how I could meet him. What was the other option? How I could reach him? I was restless. Something stroked my mind. I rushed to my home. I told Eesha not to worry. I told her that I would return soon. I asked her to take care of herself. I drove my car very fast. I reached home.

My mom opened the door. Before she could ask something, I ran into my room and I was searching files. After struggling for few minutes I was able to find the trek list. I had developed a habit of jotting down personal information of all the members on a paper even though it was also saved in my laptop.

I found my Rajgad trek file and I found there Aryan's address. I tore papers which had his information and ran. I ran towards our parking. I folded that paper and shoved that in my pocket. I read once what address was mentioned on it. I did not know where his society was. But I have heard about that area. I started my car and followed the address. It took almost half an hour to reach. My hands were still shaking while driving. My phone was ringing. But I couldn't pick it up. I was hoping for the best. I was praying for him. I reached his area and asked few people on the way. I was glad to have reached there. I reached to the society. It was a small apartment. His flat was on 5th floor. I was in so much in hurry that I could not bear to wait for the elevator.

Finally lift came. I got in the lift. I was looking in the mirror. My eyes were red, swollen. I found myself very scared. Lift stopped. I came out and I noticed the door was locked. I tried to find something there. Then I pressed his neighbor's bell. It was late but I had no option. One old lady opened the door.

I greeted that lady and asked her lady about Aryan. I wasn't having his photo with me. I showed her address and asked her if a person called Aryan was living next door? I demanded her if she knew him.

Lady: I don't know his name, but yes one boy was living there but from so many days the door is locked. I guess he shifted somewhere else. I don't know apart from that.

Me: When did you saw him last time?

Lady: I don't remember exactly beta, but I can say so many days before.

Me: Ok aunty. Thank you.

Lady: Mention not, beta.

Then I started thinking, where he had gone? What had happened with him? Many negative thoughts were crowding my mind. It was getting hard to digest. Some time before as I had tried his number and it was switched off. I even searched at the address mentioned by him. But he had already shifted somewhere else few days back. I didn't know what was happening? Where could I find him?

I returned to Eesha's home empty handed. Sid and Eesha were waiting for me in the living room. They inquired what had happened and I told them everything. Eesha was numb and did not know how to react. I was thinking about him, and more I thought I was clueless where he might be. But he was wrong. He had not even contacted me once after he had gone away on that night. It was such a pleasant night for me. We were having our first night walk together. I was enjoying his company. I was about to confess my love for him.

Suddenly he got a call and asked me to excuse him. When he disconnected the call, he apologized and told me that he would be going for some urgent work. And he went away. From that day he didn't contact me yet. Why? What would be the reason?

So many days passed away. I didn't find Aryan. One month passed. I had joined my new company. Everything was going nicely. Sid also joined his new company. Eesha had recovered more than what we had expected. I was happy for her. My routine has started. I was enjoying my new work, projects. But whenever I was little free, I could not stop myself from thinking about Aryan.

Was he dead or alive?

The Hidden Face

I was soon fed up of regular routine. I wanted to do something different in my life but my mind was not working properly. I had many things to do. But each time something happened, I could not stop myself thinking about what Eesha had told me about Aryan. However much I tried hard but I could not control my mind. Imagining her burnt body sent shiver through my spine. I believed myself to be a strong girl but that time I couldn't help it.

Every day, every night I was only thinking about Eesha and Aryan. How she was doing now, the question came to my mind. And I didn't find Aryan yet. Where was he? Was he gone far away from me? Why there was no contact between us? Was he alive or not?

Many unanswered questions were fucking my mind.

Eesha wasn't sure about Aryan. She felt that she saw Aryan near bakery on that uneventful day. But my mind and heart was not accepting whatever Eesha was saying. And even she was not 100% sure. I was having my worst days in my life since one month. I was feeling like as if a life was playing a big game with me. But what I could do? I have searched everywhere but I could not find a trace of him. That wasn't my fault. Why I am so tensed? Why was I always thinking about him? If he loved me then he will contact me. If he did not love me then he would find another girl. Why should I worry about him? If he cared then he would definitely contact me.

You are not sure whether your love is waiting for you or not. But sometimes it comes to you when you least expect it. And once it comes; you feel like as if your life is shining like sunshine and it's a feeling like as if you want to touch the sky in an excitement. You don't even notice it when your partner's wishes and dreams become yours. You feel like you have entered in a new world where no one exists except your love. And you want to begin to cherish every moment with your love. You should know when your partner needs you and at that time you have to be with your partner. It comforts the relation. I have seen that true love between Sid and Eesha.

They were truly made for each other. And I wanted the some commitment in my life. But from whom am I expecting it all this? Who had not even cared to know? Only once I would get connect with Aryan, then I will confess him what actual feeling I had for him. I don't know what will it bring but I wanted him to get to know about me and my love for him. I wanted to tell him that I would love to spend my rest of life with him.

But now I needed to be very strong and had to move on my passionate treks for the sake of Eesha. In summer, I would be arranging a trek in Manali. Many people had suggested me that place. I opened up my MH-trek club's website and in other tab I had opened my Gmail account to check mails. So that I shall get to know who all had requested me to arrange treks.

And so I could arrange the best trek this time.

I typed my Gmail ID and password. I hate it when loading a page takes so much time. I was scrolling the mails to get the details of my friends and to differentiate their suggestions. But after 48 mails when I scrolled to next page I found one mail that had a different subject mentioned. It was only two words "Hi Me". I got confused. First I ignored that mail. I thought it must be advertising mail or it might be any newsletter subscription. The sender had not even mentioned his or her name. I didn't know what that was. I neglected that mail and scrolled down further to check other mails. When I finished the work, before closing the tab I gave it a thought and went again to the 2nd page to read that mail. I was thinking whether to open that mail or not.

I arranged my paperwork neatly in a folder as it would help me to work without any hassle. I kept my folder on study table and went into the kitchen as I needed to drink plenty of water. I made a cup of hot coffee for me and then came back to read the unread mail. I didn't know whether it was important for me or not. But I thought to read it at once.

I opened the mail. There was too much matter written in the mail as if any director has sent me a film story. And as if my task was to properly map the journey of character before going about casting the actors. It was too much. I fed up just looking at the screen by actually imagining how much it would be difficult for me to read. But I told myself to read it at once. When I read all the matter I was stunned. I couldn't believe it for a while. I didn't know if it was true or not. I was totally lost my senses. I was heartbroken. I had shudders in my body. I was almost in tears and my heart broke into pieces.

Truth that was hidden...

Hi Pallavi,

"I don't know from where I should start. But it needs lot of guts to accept your fault. And I guess I shouldn't have asked you for forgiveness but I hope you will understand me. I have gone very far away from you where you wouldn't able to find me. You were the first person in Pune to whom I have talked with. I know it would not be possible for you to forgive me. But please accept the truth that I am sharing with you.

First of all, I wanted to say thanks for those moments you spent with me. Rather, I knew that I have no right to apologize for the mistake I made. To be frank, that if you would have been there in place of me, you would definitely have done the same mistake that I did. But it was my good fortune that I was chosen for this task.

You don't know where your love is waiting for you and you don't even know where your love takes you to. Since the day I first met you I was getting closer to the humanity, love, happiness. But your misfortune couldn't save you from all this. I realized that I had started developing feelings for you but it was worthless to share with. I am a wrong person to come in your life. In fact, you deserve a better person. Not me. The wholly shit!

While reading this email, don't ever think about me, because I am not your Aryan. Aryan wasn't my real name, it was a fake one. Today 13 Feb. 2010 is my last day of life.

I know, when you will read this mail I wouldn't be there as I have committed suicide; I didn't know whether it was my right or wrong decision. I just did it for my sake. This was the biggest truth that I hid it from you which I thought of sharing with you now.

I don't know what and how to tell you; what I have felt for you; how many times I have desired to be with you. I knew how I have stopped myself for having a thought of spending a quality time with you. I have felt your feelings but I never accepted it but never ever had any possibility to express it to you. I was never meant for anyone. That's the truth I couldn't ever bear. Not only in anyone's life but also in relationships there were consequences and misfortunes waiting to happen. No one's love story is as perfect as we imagine in the picture or in dreams.

I enjoyed the trek. It was an amazing experience. I find myself attached to nature again. You have thought that I might be a new comer as a trekker, but I was showing you that I was unknown to all this things. I was collecting information about the city albeit unknowingly from you. I was bonded to my work. I felt your infatuation towards me. I already had a lot of information about your city. Even after having spent time with you over there at the same known places that I already had planned to visit before my death. The day when I went to German Bakery with you, I couldn't able to recognize what I really wanted to. I was quiet. And next time unfortunately I found you there with your friends inside the bakery. I left the thought to go there.

I had been brought here in Pune, unfortunately to plant a bomb at the German bakery which would rip it apart.

I am here because of those radicals; but you're there because of you and your beloved people. Whatever you're reading is true. This was my entire fault. I was so wrong; but you tried to make me human again for a change but I had to deny it. That was my fault too. But sometimes I felt lucky that I had a chance but I had to sacrifice it for myself only.

They had locked me in a room. They were continually harassing me to agree with them. When I was brought to their territory, I was told that we had to go for work in India. They handed over the map of the area of which we were supposed to gather information. And it was the cultural capital of Maharashtra.

I will be the one responsible among those radicals who were chosen for conducting the bomb blast at German Bakery. I don't know about other mates. I know our target was to kill many including children, foreigners. But I am also dying with them. I am dying with my dreams, my hopes. I am dying for my family.

148

Now it was a big question mark flashing on your face that who were "they"?

They were the conspirators who tried to control their little worlds but I too was one of them. Their attempts to control the world and recruit others to make them radicals are really pathetic. It is these conspirators forced me to do something which I never wished to do.. I wouldn't have been one of them but unfortunately it was all planned by my destiny. I had a plan; I had a target that has forced me take this route. A far away from where I didn't yearn for. I just did it for the sake of those plotters. I had no option left but to follow their orders, it was not my initiative to target that bomb blast which unknowingly brought my end too. That's what I did to this cultural city of Maharashtra with the use of exploding a bomb. I didn't panicked when things were going according to plan but I was frightened as the plan was horrifying but there was no escape or to turn around. It was all part of the plan that I couldn't resist myself to live either. I had lost my mind, my strength. That target became my weakness.

I was introduced to a misanthrope. I had to obey the established orders from radicals and everything became chaos. I could be the misanthrope that's the only wish I couldn't have asked for. But to see my parents alive I had to take so many lives by participating conspiracy of bomb blast. Unfortunate sequences take place because life is so unfair sometimes. This is what happened when an unstoppable force meets an immovable object. I wanted to listen to my heart but was unable to escape from my mind. I could be truly incorruptible but I was left with no choice at all. Sometimes I used to think that I might have been destined to do this. One upon a time; I was one from the people who believed in good but someone played prank on me; my spirit was broken completely with no choice left.

I was brought down to their level through continual harassment. It wasn't hard for them but they used to with all their gravity. All it takes them a little switchovers between two minds. This is how they brought me to do so. They never give you choices for what they wanted you to do but also for what they don't want you to do. I couldn't ever dare to justify myself as I knew what I am paying for in my life. I couldn't even say sorry for everything. I was just trapped in the plot they created. I never thought even once that I could escape from all this as I knew there was no escape. It wasn't what I want. I survived through the ordeal they had put me into that no one could have dared to desire for. You can't live long enough to see yourself become the villain.

Sometimes, the truth isn't good enough to save yourself what you had become. People do chase their dreams and I am sulking unfortunately chasing the target that was given to me. That was my choice. I did it because not to face further consequences in my life. The night is darkest just before the dawn but there was no dawn in my life that I could desire to be waiting for.

I am far away now. It might be a better thing that I did than I have ever done. I couldn't take it; the injustice. I mean no one's ever going to know who exploded the bomb. In fact, they don't need to know it was me. After all, I never have been an immortal.

I was not a normal person with whom you could have spent life with. I was a misanthrope to whom you tried to make believe that humanity is still alive. I wasn't come here to find a love for me, but I found you who changed my thought; taught me to love and live again. I used to forget everything whenever I was with you. I was stopping myself to control my feelings, my emotions to hide from you. And that's the reason why I was being rude with you. But I never got a chance to learn how I could make myself a human being again.

Life is one time offer to chase your dreams and make them true. Very few people get opportunities to make their dream come true. Everyone has their own dreams, but many of them have failed to complete them. But lucky ones who achieve their dreams are the happiest people who never get introduced to their misfortune. But I wasn't one of them. I didn't get a second chance after I got trapped. Their sinister design trapped my dreams too. I was living in the hell.

I might have done something wrong in my past life so I had to repay it in this life. I know you won't forgive me but please don't blame yourself for this. As you will reach to the end of the mail, delete it. Erase me from your heart, from your life. I am watching you from the above. Don't ever lose your passion and do work hard for something good to make happen in your life so that I can thank my stars. I hope you'll never ever stop helping others to be happy, just like you did for me. You've a good fortune so make it as your best weapon to spread the happiness around you. Stay Blessed. Take care of yourself. Love you."

Yours Aryan…
Mail sent on 13th Feb 2010, 12.30p.m.

I sat on chair and my laptop was open on the table, after reading the mail. I did not know if it was true or not. I didn't understand for a while. I sat on chair for so many hours. I was feeling like as if I was falling unconscious. I was totally blank after reading this whole mail. I had faith in him, a blind faith. I had spent so much time with him. Why? Why I asked him to meet me for a coffee? Just Because of his diverse behavior, different lifestyle, and the one who had lost somewhere. If I could know this person is a cheater I would have never met him. Why I didn't listen to Eesha? Why I hid everything from her? What I got?

She was stopping me from meeting him, interacting with him. He was a bad guy. He was misanthrope, a murderer. He wasn't from Pune and for his sake I showed him Pune city. The time I had spent with him was unbelievable. I had spent my time with a terrorist. Was it true? Or am I fool? Why had I gone with him? I did help him indirectly. I was involved in him. This means I was responsible for Eesha's condition. I didn't know what I had done is right or wrong?

I thought myself. All I had done was bullshit. If he cared for me then he wouldn't have done this. I woke up after so many hours. I took my laptop. I didn't even change my clothes. I x didn't even comb my hair. I took the keys from my study table and went down stairs. I put my laptop in my car and drove towards.......

Regrets...

I drove towards German bakery. I parked my car in that lane. I got down from my car. I stood in front of the German bakery. Nothing was there. Floor was even clean properly. I put my first step from where the bakery starts.

I was imagining where Aryan must have sat or stood, or had he just entered the bakery and bomb went off. I was standing at the spot from where Eesha had entered the bakery and she took few steps and bomb went off. Not only German Bakery got finished in the blast but other shops were also lost or damaged that I had seen by myself. So many people were here that day.

Family members, school children, friends, senior citizens, foreigners lost their beloved or had to take care of the injured for all their life. What was the fault of those people who had to suffer unnecessarily? Those foreign nationals were guest in our country. They were enjoying their time or enjoying their holidays. The events that might have taken place prior to the blast flashed in front of my eyes. I imagined that everyone was enjoying, talking, eating or drinking something and suddenly there was a blast. In place of Eesha I should be there. Because I was with Aryan, I showed him Pune; I helped him to achieve his target. What was the fault of Eesha? Why she went there. I will be happy if I got burnt in the blast. Because of me it happened with Eesha, it happened with other people. So many people were lying here after the bomb blast. So many people were dead so many were injured. What happened with the children I can't even imagine also?

Then I left the place and drove to Eesha's home. I reached at Eesha's home. I rang the doorbell. Sid opened the door and he said hello

Pallavi, we were just…

I interrupted his words and I didn't say any word. I directly went to Eesha's room. Eesha was feeling happy. She was laughing so genuinely. I fell in front of her. I put laptop aside. She shouted Sid to come. She asked me what had happened to me. She asked if I was okay or not?

They both were shocked and were looking at me. They did not know what happened to me. They were stunned for a while. I switched on my laptop and opened my Gmail account. Sid was asking me what had happened. He asked me something was wrong in office? I didn't utter a single word. Eesha also asked me so many times but I was quiet. I opened that mail again which Aryan had sent me. I showed both of them. I put my laptop in Eesha's lap. I moved from there and sat in one corner.

They both were reading it. I noticed that Eesha glanced at me for some seconds. I didn't feeling guilty or hurt. I don't have feelings. I was totally numb due to shock.

After reading the shocking news they both were staring at me. Eesha closed the laptop and put it on the side table. Sid suddenly came near me. He took me near Eesha, where she was sat on her bed. Sid forced me to sit near her and I sat there. Eesha took my hand in hers.

Eesha: Pallavi…Look at me.

I put my head down and I was watching at the floor. I didn't have guts to make an eye contact with Eesha. After few minutes I started crying.

Me: "I am sorry Eesha, whatever you were dealing for last few days had happened because of me. He was so rude and I just went on to know the reason behind it. I couldn't stop myself from knowing him. I know Sid, Eesha had told you everything about him. I don't even want to utter his name from my mouth. I don't know that I am insane. I unknowingly helped him to know about Pune. Because of me so many people have lost their lives, so many people are half dead, some got burnt. They all also lost their lives because of me.

I helped him. I am really sorry Eesha. Whatever you both will punish I will accept it."

Eesha and Sid: Pallavi. Please stop talking this rubbish. Have you gone mad? You had done nothing wrong, don't blame yourself. You never helped him. So stop blaming yourself. This was not your fault Pallavi.

Me: No. Today because of me, Eesha, my best friend, was found in worst condition. I didn't forget this till the last breath. Anyways I wish god will punish me soon. Now I am going home, it's too late now. I hope Eesha you will forgive me. Bye. Eesha take care. Sid you too take care of her. Eesha told Sid to drop me at home. But I refused to him.

You don't come, Sid. I will be all right. Nothing will happen to me. I will text you both once I reach the home. I moved from Eesha's home and after 20 minutes I reached at my home. I informed both of them. I got freshened up. I was looking in the mirror. I was blaming that person who was in the mirror, the one who had taken her for granted. My mom called me for dinner. I sat there on the dining table. I didn't help her to arrange dishes for us. I had dinner but I was so quiet.

Mom asked me but I refused to give her reply. I finished my dinner and went to my room. I didn't even say good night to my mom & dad. They felt something went wrong but neither had they asked me nor they forced me to tell. I switched off the lights and went to sleep. I woke up at 6 a.m. in the morning. That day I had a meeting and I had to prepare some paper work for it so I got ready fast. I went to office without having breakfast properly. I reached at office. Everyone was busy in discussing with each other related to work and new projects. Today's meeting was scheduled at 3 p.m. and I had to join with my seniors. I skipped a lunch also. I was sitting quiet on the chair. Instead of checking our presentation slides I was watching my old pictures on my laptop.

Suddenly I heard someone was calling me. One employee from administration department had come to my cabin to inform me to come for a meeting. I told him, "Yes. I am coming in 5 minutes." I went in conference room. A marketing representative was giving a presentation. I wasn't concentrating on it. I found myself blaming for whatever happened with Eesha. Her face, her pain all were coming in front of my eyes.

My mind wasn't working properly. Suddenly someone asked me, "How was it madam?" I pretended as if I saw and said, "Yes, it's nice. We have to think over it. We will discuss and make a good deal."

I immediately left the conference hall. That day, I didn't do any work. I left office that day as early as I was not feeling well. My mind wasn't able to concentrate on any things. I didn't go home. I parked my moped near in the lane no. 4 at Koregaon Park. I sat on footpath. People were looking at me. But, I didn't care about them. I was thinking when Eesha burned her body in bomb blast, how much pain she went through. Her every cell was paining at the time of surgery, post-surgery. She couldn't even walk properly for few months. Why? Just because of Aryan, it happened.

She suffered a lot because of him, because of a terrorist. How could he do this? Eesha never gave him trouble; she didn't even talk with him, then why he troubled her? He broke me too. I had feelings for that guy, who had taken so many lives. He didn't even know what friendship is, what relation is and what love is. How it could happen? How a person can have feelings for terrorist? I found myself feeling so much intolerable. I didn't know when it happened with me. I was sitting there for so many hours and watching at the German Bakery. I realized that from morning I haven't checked my mobile. Then I opened my wallet and took out cell phone from that. I saw there were 35 missed calls from Eesha and Sid.

I called Sid, *"I was driving so couldn't pick your call. I will reach at home in half an hour."*

I cut the call without listening what Sid was trying to say. I got up and reached home. I had messaged both of them Sid & Eesha that I had reach home safely. Then next day I didn't go to office. I was sitting quite in my room. I was alone in the home. Doorbell rang. I saw from the eye of the door. Sid was there. I didn't open the door. He had ranged the bell for many times but still I didn't open the door. I wasn't ready to open and to listen.

I went to office next day. My senior shouted at me because of delay in my work. That project was given to other person after considering my low performance level. I was totally working like a machine. I was following instructions only. I wasn't sharing my thoughts & ideas because my mind wasn't working properly. I accepted to keep quiet all the time. I have decided not to talk without reason with anyone. It was all unwanted days I was paying for because of his mistake which I won't forget till the last breath.

Days seemed to be like without sunrise. Night wasn't shining as the stars lost their places. I had stop arranging treks. I had stop communicating with friends. Everyone was thinking that I must be busy in work. But only Sid & Eesha knew the truth. I didn't meet them in past few days. I was running away from both of them. I didn't have courage to make an eye contact with Eesha. I have lost all my feelings, control on my mind. I do care about Eesha but.

After that day when I went to her home to reveal Aryan's secret, I didn't went at Eesha's home to see her. How she is feeling now? Is she fine? She needs me but I am not there with her. I remembered what doctor had told me (Eesha needs me. So be with her as much as you can). I was asking to Sid about Eesha's health via messages. Whenever I do message him, he asks me what's wrong with me. And I didn't answer him. I had lost so many projects due to my deplorable performance level in my office.

One day, I was going home after finishing my office work, I found Sid in my home. He was sitting with my mother. He gave me a strange look. I just waved him a "Hi" and went in my room. He followed me in my room. He told me to come at Eesha's home. And I refused him again. I had so much work of my project. He urged me to come thrice but I didn't listen to him. Sid held my hand so tightly and he took me at Eesha's home forcefully. He put me in his car and we headed towards Eesha's home. I was standing at the entrance of her room.

I glanced at Eesha. She was doing exercise of her hand. She was happy that she can move her hand freely. I saw her and my eyes filled with tears. I suddenly wiped my tears & entered her the room. I sat near Eesha. She didn't even look at me. She was looking away.

Me: Eesha. Please look at me.

Eesha: Why I should look at you? You don't care who I am. You didn't come to meet me for past few weeks. If you don't want to talk to me then I am not going to force myself.

Me: I am sorry. I was feeling restless thinking about you. Because of me you are paying for what you don't have to.

Eesha: I told you many times that you aren't responsible for what I am going through.

Me: Yes I am responsible for it.

Eesha: Pallavi. Please stop blaming yourself damn it. You have done so much for me Pallavi. Even I can't imagine to blame you in my dreams. You are very strong girl. You faced very difficult situation in your life. Stop blaming yourself. It's not the right thing to wipe someone's mistake. He played with everyone. He didn't care who should live who shouldn't. He did it for his parents so they could live.

Do you think his parents might be alive till yet? I don't think so. He thinks that he had done for his parents. No way. He did it because he wanted to escape from his life. To escape he had no option either except succeeding the target. It wasn't your mistake Pallavi You didn't put a gun on his head and forced him to do bomb blast. You have taught him how to live. You have taught him to live passionately. But he couldn't himself because it wasn't written on his destiny. He was the only one responsible for whatever had happened, not you my dear.

Eesha wiped my tears. She held my hand. I felt liberated from the burden. She continued.

Eesha: I have deleted his mail from your account. That day you had forgotten your laptop at my place. I read that mail again and at that time I deleted it. If I would not have done that then you would have definitely read that mail for many times. Pallavi, please don't behave like this. You don't know how scared we were thinking about you. And dear we care a lot for you. And start to live your life with passion once again. Don't live like a machine that needs commands to work?

Me: I wasn't in a condition to talk with anyone. Thoughts were eating up my mind from inside. I didn't know when I will get over from it after happening so much with me. I knew that someday you both will come to me.

If I wouldn't meet him so much then I didn't had faced this problem ever. He was rude so I helped him to live peacefully. This was my big fault. Because of him everyone suffered through it. The main thing you have suffered a lot which is the truth and pain. You almost spend your days in a terrible condition which nobody could see this. The truth will never change that I had strong feelings about him, a misanthrope.

3 years passed away. Eesha was absolutely normal and she had got a job too. Sid had joined his family business. And I was repairing day by day.

I started meeting new people to boost my confidence, to promote my passionate treks. I had become a senior administrator in my company and it's just because of Sid & Eesha only. If they weren't with me then my life would had become like a mud. And now I am getting engaged with the one whom I am sharing my all the past. Just because I wanted to build trust in our relation and I wanted to be clear and transparent. I don't know it might affect your decision or not but I wanted to share this all from past few days.

Our Engagement...

That was the happiest day in my life. The change in my life brought a good opportunity for me to walk on a new track to fulfill the journey of love and happiness. Once again I was ready to allow myself to soak in the romance and begin my new life. I was not satisfied with the decision that had taken, but somewhere you need to accept the opportunity that life is giving to you for the second time. Those opportunities do not easily come in everyone's life.

Suddenly a voice came from behind that was my mom. "Beta, what are you doing there? Still you didn't get ready?"

When I heard my mom's voice, immediately I wiped off my tears and stand to face in front of my mom and said, "Wait mom, I am getting ready. Give me some more time. Send Eesha to my room if she has come. I need her help in getting ready fast."

Mom: Okay beta, but be ready within 15-20 minutes as ceremony will start soon. We have to reach the venue as soon as possible.

Me: Yes Mom. I know.

When I forced my mom to go down, at that time she gave me a little bit weird look and went away. I wore a bottle green colored sari with red mix golden border and some gold accessories. I watched myself in the mirror. I was smiling. Forcefully. I was entering in my new life. Once upon a time I wasn't even keeping trust on anyone. And now I am getting engaged with the person whom I didn't know completely. I don't know if I will fell in love with him or not. But I will fulfill his all wishes. I don't know whether I will tell him the truth or not.

Someone knocked the door and I opened. Eesha and Sid were there. I was happy after seeing them. We three hugged very tightly. And almost tears came in my eyes. Eesha gave me a kiss on my cheek and said she loves me. Those words are still special for me. I hadn't applied make up. Eesha told me to keep a natural look. They were teasing me to create my mood.

Rohan is an Owner of **IDEL** Pvt. Ltd. a company that deals in Import-Export business. His aims and honesty made him successful in his life. He successfully settled up his business after his masters. Pallavi had never thought of getting a guy like him.

They were saying Rohan is so lucky for having a girl like Pallavi in his life. We left from our home and headed towards The Westin, a grand five rated hotel in Koregaon Park where our engagement ceremony was held. I was passing through the place where bomb-blast had taken place 3 years ago. But today I had seen German Bakery was undergoing a renovation. Once again it will be the best place to hangout. But memories are still burning. Some faces are still missing which are impossible to reborn. I looked at Eesha and held her hand very tightly. She sensed it why. A drop of a tear came from her left eye. And she slightly wiped it.

Later I found that place where Aryan left me alone that night. I was calling him continuously, but he switched off his phone and I was unable to reach at him. I wanted to tell him about the feelings I have for him. But I couldn't. I was waiting there. I thought he will come back. But he didn't. I wish whatever I had experienced in my life that would never come again.

The function was the reason which brought happiness after so many days in my life, the moment I was sharing with my family, I had seen the deepest happiness in the smile that came on my parent's face. This function means a lot for them. They are very happy for me, but I am pretending smiling face in front of my parents and still confused about the decision I have taken for my family's happiness. But here I am missing those some memories to the core.

Those memories still give me a lot of pain which I am trying to erase always from my mind, my heart. I reached at Westin I was coming with my whole family.

All people were watching at me in the function. The most awaited person at the function was Rohan; who were almost fell in love with me. And for a change, I was sincerely agreed to accept your love. That day, you were looking smart than before when I looked you for the first time in formals. You had worn off white colored Kurta and maroon color silk dhoti. I noticed you; you were continuously looking at me. I broke eye contact with you. And I went to meet your mom-dad. I took blessings from them and sat beside you who were still looking at me.

Later, when panditji was busy in murmurs mantra and all and afterwards he told you to begin to wear a ring in his fiancé's finger. Before wearing a ring you looked straight in my eyes and gave a lovely smile which little bit give comfort to me for accepting the ring. And unexpectedly this time I gave a real smile. You held my hand very softly. And when I was wearing a ring on your finger, you were definitely expecting a cute smile from me and I managed somehow for you.

Someone announced that they both exchanged their rings. When no one was noticing us, then you gave a compliment to me in a low voice so that no one could hear. He said that today I was looking beautiful. You were showing me your madness about me, your love for me, making me little bit scared, if I will not love you whole life than, But that time, I did not respond you well. I just put a little shy smile on my face to feel you better.

Something was pulling me back: my memories, my past. And I was not ready to go into my past, as because of it I have lost many things in my life. Everything was coming in front of my face. I wanted to tell you everything what happened with me, if you will get to know the truth, I want to tell you before our marriage. I was waiting for the right time. I don't want to break your trust, I don't want to hide things from you, because I saw genuine care and love in your eyes for me.

I saw you ones, when you came to see me in my home, as a person you were very much attractive, fair looking and well-built; any girl would die for you.

You were much suitable in your black half frame spectacles and having little faint French cut made you look impressive. You were sitting on the sofa, beside your father and mother. You were in formals. I just once looked at you, you were staring at me. I wore a white and faint blue Punjabi dress. Immediately, I broke eye contact with you. Then, I sat in front of everybody. I was feeling uncomfortable. I was expecting rejection from your side. So that I will get some time to recover from my past.

You were like, a dream came true. And I am there not much interested in you. You tried your best to know me completely but I did not respond to you carefully when our parents told us to sit separately so that I and you would get a chance to know each other. We have hardly spoken with each other. We were talking like we are playing a quiz game. You were asking me questions and I was answering you only. I was not in mood to ask about you. I was waiting to leave from there as earliest as possible.

After rendezvous got over, while going you looked at me with your loving smile and I responded to you with a sarcastic smile. Your smile was enough to know for me whether you will accept this proposal or not. A function has changed my thoughts about you. And somehow I managed many times to bring smile on my face to feel him better. When I met you so many times i slowly get to know about your behavior, your care, your love about me, changing my thinking about you. That day the happiest day for everyone who attended the function. I was not considering myself to be ever happy again. All that happiness belongs to those people who are really worthy of it.

Finally the function got over. You were leaving. You were looking at me and waved at me with your lovely smile. Your lovely smile always said something to me. There was something behind your smile and it's a feeling of fullness. And I loved it. But I was not much more eager to know. But I liked it. Next day I woke up and I saw my mobile, and there were 5 missed calls and 3 unread messages. All were from you, so I called you.

While talking over the phone I was comfortable. I was wishing I could feel comfortable like this when I would tell you about my past. After some time, I went downstairs and my family was busy having breakfast. That time everybody was teasing me with your name. I remembered your smiling face whenever you looked at me. Surprisingly I started liking you. But really am I?

Present Day - Sharing truth

We decided to meet many times in past days. Today, I texted you while leaving. And I was thinking to tell you everything today itself. But I don't know from where I should start. We almost met for before 3-4 times but I didn't' even utter a single word about my past which I wanted to share with you. I was feeling guilty. Now I have told you everything what I felt about you, about my past, about Aryan, about Eesha. Those things I wanted to share with you before our marriage. Now you can tell me your decision, what you think about me. Have I done right or wrong? Please tell me whatever you had in your mind. I wanted to know everything.

While narrating my past to him I could stop myself from crying. There was silence in the café. Some were staring at us. Rohan sat near me. He gave me his handkerchief. He didn't stop me from crying. He wanted me to vent out all my emotions, regrets so that I would feel light. Rohan ordered one glass of water for me. I drink water and put the glass on a table. I stopped crying. I was feeling like a free bird. It was a feeling like as if my mind has lost so many loads.

He took a pause and said, "Pallavi still you have feelings about Aryan. I don't think you will overcome from it. I think we can't spend whole life together. You need more time to get out from this. You need to rethink over our relation before it's too late. I didn't expect this from you. You should have told me before our engagement. I guess that ring in your finger shouldn't be for you.

He took my left hand and removed my ring from a finger. He got up from couch and left from there. I didn't believe this for a while.

I took a last sip of coffee. I was stunned by his behavior was a little bit strange but I am responsible for it. Just before some time I had narrated him my story. He consoled me but he went. I am alone. He took my engagement ring before leaving. I was least expecting this from him. But I was clueless. I broke down and tears were rolling down from my eyes. I was like as if sand slipping through my hand and I am watching it helplessly. I looked behind to find out if he had left me alone forever or was it just my illusion. But he was not there. It was all over. I have lost everything. I was feeling like all my happiness got finished. I couldn't help it. I was scared.

I thought to leave from there. I don't have to feel bad for this. I think it might help us to keep trust on each other for the rest of our life.

But

I returned to life. When I got up from couch, I turned to live. I was stunned. Oh My God...

I was shocked. Rohan was walking towards me with a lovely smile on his face which I had seen on our engagement. I don't know what he was doing. He came closer to me. I was quiet. It's unbelievable for me which I will never ever forget that moment. That was the reason he told me to give him back the ring. He wanted to propose me again by wearing that ring. That's what means he wanted to marry with me. He softly took my hand in his hand and he wore a ring.

Rohan

"Pallavi, I have already decided at the time of our engagement that whatever past may be, I will be with you till the last breath. I feel proud to you have in my life. The way you have faced in every

situation. The situation you have handled so bravely. I know you still care about Eesha, from the pressure and burnt memory you gone through. I know it was very difficult for you, but you faced it very bravely. I feel so lucky to have you. You will support me in every difficult situation.

I fallen in love with you since the day I met you. I found myself melted looking at your cute smile. It was like a true love I have never felt before. I want to find the light in your eyes. I want to find a way by your side. I want to fill your heart with love. For me, it was pleasure being loved by you. I will be the person who can separate you from your memories; worst days you ever had.

I Love You Pallavi. Will you marry me?"

It was very tough to believe him. When he expressed his feelings like I was integral part of his life. When he held my hand the feeling was amazing filled with pride. Once again with tears in my eyes I was listening to him honestly. How can he easily accept me after knowing the truth and what about my future?

In today's life, it's difficult to move on without disclosing the truth and hidden secrets to save yourself from spoiling your relation. But, what life brings in your path, we have to accept it. We need to hope that someday situation will change.

He was unbelievable. How he could do this. Whatever he decided was just to see me happy, to wipe out my bad memories. He was like a new wave coming to a sea shore, which is helping me to erase the footprints left behind. a loving person. After listening to his few words I realized that love is not about doing something but it's about believing someone deeply. Still thinking about his honesty, his love.

I said, "Yes Rohan. I love you too."

We hugged. I said those three magical words in his ears again and gave kiss on his cheek. We left from there. Everyone was looking at us.

Epilogue

Siddharth and Eesha, both are happy as they are getting engaged soon. I & Rohan got married. We both are so much happy with each other that nothing can do us apart. I feel the strongest relation on the earth that is to rise in love with your charming prince.

Love is the hardest thing anyone can experience in life, but it's the best feeling anyone can ever have.

Memories are the best part of our life which reminds us about the time we had spent with someone and who knows that those times will come again or not. Memories are which sometimes gives relief to our heart and sometimes pain also.

A person with a broken heart needs some more time to recover from their past with the supporting and caring hand. It will build trust in you and who knows some day, maybe you will have that thing in your hand which you were waiting for. Sometimes, we lose something which might be the reason for something more beautiful than that what is exactly waiting in our life. Be patient. Life goes on, it never ends.

Printed in the United States
By Bookmasters